CHOCOLATE MILK, X-RAY

AND → ME

CHOCOLATE MILK, X-RAY SPECS AND ME

BETHANY WALKER

Illustrated by JACK NOEL

SCHOLASTIC

Published in the UK by Scholastic Children's Books, 2021
Euston House, 24 Eversholt Street, London, NW1 1DB, UK
A division of Scholastic Limited.

London – New York – Toronto – Sydney – Auckland
Mexico City – New Delhi – Hong Kong

Text © Bethany Walker, 2021
Illustration © Jack Noel, 2021

The right of Bethany Walker and Jack Noel to be identified as the
author of this work and illustrator has been asserted by them under
the Copyright, Designs and Patents Act 1988.

ISBN 978 0702 30280 0

A CIP catalogue record for this book is available from the British Library.

Printed
Papers

This is a wo
and dialogues
fictitiously.
ev

CLASSIFIEDS

To Robin, Elsie and Lonnie. With all my love.

OR SALE

★ ★ ★ ★ ★ ★

COMPANY SEEKS SPROUT LOVER

Have you considered being a sprout farmer? If you love to work in the field and enjoy travel, this could be the job you seek! Just solve this clue to apply:

EQDCCXHRFQDZS

Mr and Mrs Spicer
The International Federation of Sprout Farmers
11353
Outer Castonga

March 30

Dear Mum and Dad,

Have you arrived in **OUTER CASTONGA** yet? I hope your journey went well. I'm still GUTTED that I couldn't come with you - are you ABSOLUTELY sure I can't join you?

It sucks that you've had to go away so soon after we've moved here. And who cares about farming SPR🥬UTS? I mean, what's the worst that could happen: _no sprouts_? I wish you were still cabbage-farming in Norfolk - at least then we were all together.

1

And why did you have to go away during the Easter holidays? There's NO ONE around to play with. You remember Ajay Coppertoe? Like us, he's only just moved here and we started school at the same time? Well, Ajay is the _one_ friend I've made since we moved here and he's on holiday with his dad, so the only person I've got to hang out with is Grandad. It's really boring.

I've been working hard on my Easter project. It was so nice of Lamont Riley to tell me about it. Lamont normally barely speaks to me. I can't believe I missed Mr Norbert's announcement to the class about the Easter project when I went off to the loo. Lamont _went out of his way_ to tell me all about the project. So nice of him! A 5,000 word essay on the history of pencils seems like a strange project to set – and it doesn't link with anything we've been learning at school – but at least it's something to do!

At EVERY meal, Grandad is feeding me sprouts. YUCK! Just because we get them free! I know you said, "A day without sprouts is a day without sunshine," but I'd be quite happy with a gazillion days of rain if it meant I didn't have to eat sprouts!

Better go. It's time for my chocolate milk. But Grandad always stirs the powder in. It's soooooo much better how you do it - shaken, not stirred.

love

Freddy

P.S. I tried to find **OUTER CASTONGA** on our globe but couldn't see it. It must be a very small country.

Freddy Spicer
61 Bond Lane
Fleming
Flemingshire
BR0 CL1

April 4

Dearest Freddykins,

We have arrived safe and well in **Outer Castonga**. What rotten luck that you are severely allergic to Castongan Pine Spores! The ~~completely real~~ doctor you saw was quite adamant that it was too risky for you to come with us. We can't have our little Freddybobs getting sick! Conditions here are ~~dangerous~~ tough so it is probably a good job that you have stayed home with Grandad.

   Our ~~mission~~ task to introduce new sprout farming techniques to **the farmers of Outer Castonga** should be simple enough and we'll be back before you know it.

In the meantime:
- Make sure Grandad looks after you
- Stay out of the study and away from our special gardening equipment in the shed

1

- Eat your sprouts. They are nature's gobstoppers.

Sending you big hugs and kisses.

Lots of love,
Mummy and Daddy

Mr and Mrs Spicer
The International Federation of Sprout Farmers
11353
Outer Castonga

April 6

Dear Mum and Dad,

School has now started back after the Easter hols but
the WORST thing has happened... Ajay has suddenly
left!! After just one term! How come the ONE friend
I'd made at Fleming School has

already   moved   away?
It's rubbish. There's a
rumour that Ajay's dad,
Mr Coppertoe, was last
seen being carried away
by a shark while holidaying

on a super-yacht but <u>no one really believes that.</u>

I'm dead upset - I loved playing hide-and-seek with Ajay.
And Mr Coppertoe had all this fancy computer equipment
that he allowed Ajay and me to play on. There were
so many strange devices - our favourite game was
pretending Ajay's dad was an enemy spy. I know we'd
only been at school together for a term but Ajay was
my best friend and it's sooooooo pants that I'm starting
my second term without him. ~~I was looking forward to~~
~~not being the friendless new boy for a change but I'm~~
~~right back at square one.~~

Now I have to start all over again and make new
friends. There's one boy who seems OK in my class,
called Lamont Riley. Lamont is the smallest boy in the
year but he's really loud to make up for it. And he has
the most amazing eyebrows - like two slugs dancing
on his forehead! He's the one who told me about the

Easter project - but I think Lamont must have made a

mistake coz when I handed my project in, Mr Norbert

said there was no Easter project. But Mr Norbert gave

me a smiley face for effort AND I now know that the

oldest known pencil is from the Seventeenth Century,

so it wasn't a total waste of time.

Lamont plays for the football team so I thought I'd

give that a go. I "tried out" for the team but all that

running made me feel like I was going to explode - it's

those blummin SPROUTS ! I was just about to

score but as I took aim, I knew I was about to PARP, so I

stopped to let the feeling pass AND THEN Maya Peterson

stole my shot and got a team place instead. SO UNFAIR! I

bet she doesn't have to eat sprouts every day.

How is OUTER CASTONGA ? I wish I was

with you. Should I be worried about my allergy to Castongan Pine Spores here? I told Mr Norbert about it so it could go on my school medical record but he just said, "That's not a thing." Teachers don't always know everything, do they?

Hurry up and come back.

Love

Freddy

P.S. Have you ever tried eating mashed sprouts? THEY ARE DISGUSTING!!!!!!!!!

Freddy Spicer
61 Bond Lane
Fleming
Flemingshire
BR0 CL1

April 10

Dearest Freddykins,

What a shame about your friend, Ajay – and poor Mr Coppertoe! Don't be too disheartened, though, and do keep trying to make new friends. Lamont sounds nice. How clever of you to think about joining a club! Sport has never really been our little Freddy-Weddy-Woo's thing. What about something else, like knitting? Or origami? Or model railway building?

   We feel terrible leaving you, but trying to make friends is the best thing you can be doing. And don't forget Grandad will be feeling lonely too as he doesn't know many people there either. You can always spend time with that lovely ~~agen~~ woman over the road, Desiree Delicata. She's very caring and will be glad to help you out if you need anything.

Sorry this letter is brief. We're loving receiving your letters. I know it's a pain that we can't email but ~~we just cannot rely on the security of the internet~~ there is no internet provision in Outer Castonga.

Got to go – urgent ~~International Esp~~ sprout matters to attend to.

Lots of Love,

Mummy and Daddy

Mr and Mrs Spicer
The International Federation of Sprout Farmers
11353
Outer Castonga

April 13

Dear Mum and Dad,

Thanks for your ~~short~~ letter. But can you just call me
Freddy? Enough with the Freddykins and Freddy-Weddy-
Woo. I am nearly ten, not four!! And it can have <u>serious</u>
consequences. I wasn't thinking and called Lamont
"Lamonty-Wonty-Woo" yesterday and he completely
laughed in my face. And then he told EVERYONE in class
VERY LOUDLY. How am I supposed to make friends with
him or anyone now?

  I've asked around about different clubs. Lamont told

me there was a club in the hall every Monday where you can make long stands and big weights, which sounded interesting so I went to check it out. I was standing around waiting for AGES but no one turned up. ~~It got really lonely.~~ I think Lamont must have got the day wrong.

I do have a new after-school activity, though. Mr Norbert has said I need extra help with maths. So every Tuesday, I'll be doing *MAGICAL MONSTER MATHS* for two hours. SO LAME! There's nothing magical or monstery about it. The one good thing is that Lamont is also in the group and we're going to sit together.

It's funny you wrote about Desiree Delicata in your last letter - she suddenly popped round yesterday with

a freshly baked cake, which was DELICIOUS! She said she'd check in on us from time to time to make sure we're OK. Isn't that nice? Why does she always wear really flowery dresses, though? She looks like a flower shop has thrown up on her!

Hurry up and get your job done.

love

Freddy - (NOT Freddykins, not Freddy-Weddy-Woo and not even Freddly-Beddly-Bob)

P.S. I can't find Captain Cuddles. You know I struggle to sleep without him. Did you move him?

P.P.S. The Fred-Meister is acceptable.

Freddy Spicer
61 Bond Lane
Fleming
Flemingshire
BR0 CL1

April 15

Dearest Freddykins,

Our important **sprout** work is going well in Outer Castonga but we are missing you so very much.

We're so glad you're getting help with maths. Numbers are so important. You were always much better at writing, though, and we enjoy your letters very much. Is there any club you could do with writing? Maybe don't ask Lamont about more clubs – it sounds like he enjoys pulling your leg!! We love how trusting you are, but don't let people take advantage of you!

It's nice that Desiree is looking out for you. Don't hesitate to call on her, day or night. And yes, her flowery dresses are quite something, aren't they?

We <u>promise</u> we'll be back before your birthday in June.

Be thinking what you might like to do.

Love and hugs from

Mummy and Daddy

Mr and Mrs Spicer
The International Federation of Sprout Farmers
11353
Outer Castonga

April 18

Dear Mum and Dad,

A ~~really awful embarrassing horrid~~ thing happened
this week. There's a boy in my year called Jordan
Fishwick. He is REALLY tough - you don't want to mess
with him. He always has his hair slimed down over his
eyes so you never know whether he's actually looking
at you. Jordan's obsessed with making online videos of
him pushing people over - he gets LOADS of views! Well,
this week Jordan tried to push me over, but instead he
just pushed lots of sprout wind out of me. He looked so
disgusted I thought he was going to squash me like a

maggot - but no! He just shouted, "Aw, that's disgusting, Freddy-Farty-Pants," and now the video is online. #freddyfartyPants is <u>the most popular video uploaded</u> in the history of the school. So more kids at Fleming School know who I am but it's <u>not</u> helping me make friends.

I blame SPROUTS - I wouldn't be windy and stinky if <u>you did something else.</u> Why don't you farm something tasty like oranges or chocolate? Or can you forget farming all together? I know! You could go work for Ma Teeny's Chocolate Milk Company! Then you could demonstrate to the whole world how to shake up the chocolate milk to get the mixture just right. Wouldn't it be awesome if you got free chocolate milk as a perk of your job, rather than FREE SPROUTS ?? I'd be able to bathe in chocolate milk! Even with Grandad feeding me them at EVERY meal. there's FAR TOO MANY sprouts for just me and him to get through.

Our house is starting to smell like a sprout farm. And so am I. ~~I wouldn't want to be friends with #freddyfartypants either.~~

Can you ask your work to send us fewer sprouts each week? Or even NO sprouts? Maybe when you ask your work to let you come home FOR MY BIRTHDAY!!!!

Which reminds me ... I've decided what I want to do for my birthday...

Wait for it... The BLAST YOURSELF BONKERS

LASER GAME!!!!!
Ta-da!

It's a GENIUS idea because it will be an AMAZING way to make friends. EVERYONE talks about it but NO ONE has been - it's the "Number One Hottest Ticket in Town!!!" It would be SO COOL if I could invite people there for my birthday. I'd be the most popular kid in school! (Or they might at least forget about the online video). Freddy-farty-Pants? _Freddy-Smarty-Pants._ more like. Please say you'll do this - my future happiness depends on it!

Did you know we were getting a new next-door neighbour? An old woman has just moved in. I've only seen her from a distance but she has bright red lips and very dark eyes. Grandad said she looks very "glamorous". She was wearing a very tight dress with a snake pattern on it - it looked like a snake had just swallowed a woman whole and was still digesting her. Is that glamorous?

I will look into writing clubs at school - it's a good idea ~~but I've been so embarrassed by the online video that I've been hiding for most of this week.~~ It would be nice to have something else to focus on. Lamont told me that there is an amazing "underwater chess" club in the sports hall, which transforms into a swimming pool on Wednesdays. I got ready and went along but it turns out it was just a regular chess club, which I ended up joining in my swimming trunks. It was really chilly! I think you were right about Lamont "pulling my leg". I have to stop believing what he tells me!

Love

Freddy

P.S. I was hoping Ajay Coppertoe might have written to me. I don't even know where he's moved to and I miss him.

National
Institute for
Criminal
Enterprises

To: **Dr Alpha Bett, Director**

From: **Operative A**

Date: April 19

Re: Mission "Missile Code Retrieval"

Dr Bett –

Are you sure the intelligence is correct?

You have requested 24hr surveillance on what appears to be a **perfectly normal family**: very ordinary boy and his grandad left behind in family home while the parents are working away. Only unusual issue to report is an unnatural obsession with sprouts.

Do you wish the operation to continue? I don't understand what I am doing here.

Why do you need my considerable skills?
Why am I stuck here in **nowheresville**?

Please confirm

Operative A (Lead Operative)

Freddy Spicer
61 Bond Lane
Fleming
Flemingshire
BR0 CL1

April 21

Dearest Freddy,

Sorry to hear about the viral video. By the time you receive this letter, we're sure it will have blown over and been forgotten about. I know it is tricky but you are a lovely, kind and sensitive boy, and everyone should want to be friends with you. Maybe try *talking* to that Jordan Fishwick? If you become his friend, he won't be mean to you. Remember, there's often a reason why people are horrid to others.

Here in **Outer Castonga**, we are working together, training and ~~intelligence~~-gathering for what is to come. Judging by the current climate, there's trouble brewing and everyone is expecting a super-busy **sprout** season. Writing regular letters may become more tricky.

The "Blast Yourself Bonkers" Laser Game sounds wonderful. What a super way for you to make new friends! As a special birthday treat, we promise we'll take you and some friends there. What fun!

Love and hugs from

Mummy and Daddy

Mr and Mrs Spicer
The International Federation of Sprout Farmers
11353
Outer Castonga

April 23

Dear Mum and Dad,

Thanks SO MUCH (times a million) for agreeing to take
me and some friends to *BLAST YOURSELF BONKERS* .
You're ace! It will ~~definately~~ definitely help kids see
me in a different way. By the time my birthday comes
around, maybe I'll have heard from Ajay so I could
invite him too. That would be so awesome.

   I thought about your suggestion to look for a school
club linked to writing and - guess what? There's a
Fleming School magazine! It's called **Fleming Bulletin**
but it's really tough to write for coz Head Girl Samira

Hadid is the editor and chooses what goes in. I've been told she only picks ideas by the kids in the top year. I've decided I'm going to be the first one in my year to get an article published. but Samira is really ~~beautiful~~ fussy. ~~Or maybe she just doesn't like me coz she knows I'm #freddyFartyPants~~. My first idea for an article was "*The Unknown Dangers of living with a Castongan Pine Spore Allergy*". Samira returned my article just with one comment: "That's not a thing!" I think she must have spoken to Mr Norbert about it.

I'm actually enjoying the after-school

MAGICAL MONSTER MATHS

(although I nearly missed the last session coz Lamont told me it was in a different classroom and I thought it was another one of his "jokes". Turns out he was telling the truth that time!) Whenever Mr Norbert says

ANYTHING. I just have to look at Lamont to burst out giggling. Lamont really is super funny – he can move his amazing eyebrows in almost every direction. We have a great laugh but I'm not sure the club is helping me get any better at maths!

Please can you write to Grandad and tell him we don't have to eat sprouts at EVERY meal? Seriously!! When I complain, Grandad just says, "Waste not, want not," or "Don't look a gift horse in the mouth," or "It's my war-time upbringing," and lots of other old-person sayings I don't really understand. I think they all just mean he likes free stuff and hates spending money. Yesterday he made a sprout stew – VOM!! Not even my yummy chocolate milk could take away the taste of that!

Our new neighbour is called Mrs Allbright.
She popped round (although "wiggled" is a
more accurate description – it looks very
hard to walk in those tight dresses and
high heels) to borrow some sugar, but
Grandad gave her some sprouts instead.
She did not look pleased – her bright red lips
suddenly turned all white and pursed. When
she speaks, her voice is really low and croaky.
Grandad said it is "lovely, so gravelly". Isn't
gravel like the little stones on our drive? What is lovely
about sounding like stones?

Write again soon.

Love

Freddy

To: **Operative A**

From: **Dr Alpha Bett, Director**

Date: April 24

Re: Mission "Missile Code Retrieval"

Do not question my authority, Operative A.

The last Operative who displeased me hasn't been seen since meeting my pet shark, Shirley. You do not wish to end up like Operative C, do you?

Intelligence, gained by Operative C (before **"Operation Super-Yacht Shark"**), has confirmed:

- "International Federation of Sprout Farmers" is actually the International

Espionage Agency.

- Identities of Agent Bubble and Agent Squeak have been revealed as Mr and Mrs Spicer.
- Missile Codes are known to be in possession of Agents Bubble and Squeak.

Proceed with setting up Mission "Missile Code Retrieval" as directed. Send regular reports but proceed with caution — <u>do not alert IFSF to our intelligence.</u>

Note to self: Must get an assistant. As the world's leading Criminal Mastermind, I should not have to actually be writing my own communications to my Operatives. I am far too busy and important for this.

THE RETURN OF THE WORLD'S GREATEST CRIMINAL MASTERMIND?

Reports are coming in of a number of possible sightings of the notorious Dr Alpha Bett. Dr Bett has not been seen for several years, since he attempted to kidnap the Queen of England and place himself on the throne. All recent sightings, from places as far-flung as Sydney, Sierra Leone and Slough, are as yet unconfirmed and government agencies have been refusing to speculate. It is hoped that the network of international intelligence agencies and their agents are training, co-operating and intelligence-gathering for whatever is to come. Certainly, the return of Dr Bett is bad news, whatever he is planning.

Freddy Spicer
61 Bond Lane
Fleming
Flemingshire
BR0 CL1

April 26

Dear Freddy,

We're missing you so much. Sadly, our **sprout** work has just become more challenging so we will be away for longer than we expected and we may well be out of contact for a while. We have been given the go-ahead to travel into the foothills of **Upper Outer Castonga** to continue our vital **sprout** work out in the field. We will try to write when we can – and hopefully we will be able to ring from time to time – but do try to keep busy and don't worry about us.

It's lovely to hear that you have made nice, funny friend in your maths club. But do try to concentrate as well. Remember – numbers are important! And what a shame that Samira Hadid didn't like your suggestion for a magazine article. Keep going with your ideas and don't be put off!

What about joining a school choir? You have a lovely singing voice.

We will be thinking of you. We promise to try and be back in time for your birthday and for "Blast Yourself Bonkers".

Mrs Allbright sounds like a fascinating new neighbour. Where did she move from? We'd love for you to tell us more.

Know that we are safe and well.

Lots of Love and Hugs,

Mummy and Daddy

MESSAGE FROM PROTECTION AGENT
DESIREE DELICATA TO IEA/IFSF
APRIL 26

IN POSITION AS FIRST LINE OF
PROTECTION FOR AGENT BUBBLE
AND SQUEAK'S FAMILY.

CONTACT MADE WITH FREDDY AND
MR SPICER SENIOR.

SPROUT COVER STORY INTACT.
REQUEST DETAILED SPROUT
INTELLIGENCE TO GAIN THEIR TRUST
FURTHER.

NOTHING SUSPICIOUS TO REPORT.

Mr and Mrs Spicer
The International Federation of Sprout Farmers
11353
Outer Castonga

April 29

Dear Mum and Dad,

It's rubbish I won't be getting many regular letters
from you. I look forward to them. And no one believes
me when I tell them you're in a country that doesn't
have internet provision. Who doesn't have the internet
these days! And the Outer Castongan phone lines are
terrible. Our phone calls are always USELESS - they're
so crackly, you never sound right and there's always a
weird breathing noise down the line.

There is some GOOD NEWS - I have joined "Fleming
Voices", the school choir! And I persuaded Lamont to

join too. Miss Davis, the singing teacher, is delighted
coz we're the only boys - but she's always trying to get

lamont to sing more quietly. I have to stand between

Maya Peterson and Freya Jones. They're actually really

nice and friendly but they both have so much hair that

some goes in my mouth whenever I take a breath. I

swear I'm going to end up coughing up a hairball like

a cat. The best thing is I stand behind Samira Hadid in

choir. Her hair slides down her back like a waterfall.

I can't wait for my birthday and **BLAST YOURSELF BONKERS**. I've already told Lamont about it and I could tell straight away that he thought I must be cool if I was going to take him there. I've also invited Maya and Freya - they've said they'll come if I also invite Priya Coulson. How many others can I invite? Fingers crossed I'll be able to send an invitation to Ajay too, wherever he is.

I've told Grandad how much I'm missing Ajay. I said about us playing hide-and-seek so Grandad's started playing that with me. He's not very good but it's nice to have something fun to do! I just wish he'd stop feeding me SO MANY **SPROUTS**. Thankfully, Desiree has come to the rescue a <u>tiny</u> bit and has suggested loads of different recipes that could use sprouts: sprout stir-fry, sprout gratin, sprout coleslaw, sprout risotto, sprout bubble and squeak. She knows <u>ever such a lot</u> about SPR🟢UTS! I'm pleased Grandad has taken on these suggestions but I have to tell you, he doesn't always make sprouts taste better. And HOWEVER sprouts are served up, they still have unwanted effects *if you know what I mean!*

I tried again to get an article into **Fleming Bulletin**, the school magazine – using Desiree's sprout recipes. It was called "*10 ways to hide sprouts in food*". I even suggested giving away free sprouts with each magazine but Samira Hadid is <u>very hard to impress.</u> Every time she hands an article back to me, she has this little crease above her nose. ~~It's really cute~~.

We haven't seen much more of Mrs Allbright yet so I

don't have anything new to tell you. She must be having a lot of work done to her house, though, coz there's always a big van parked outside. It's a plumber's van this week.

Try to ring soon.

Love
Freddy

P.S. Unfortunately Jordan Fishwick heard me talking about *BLAST YOURSELF BONKERS* so I've had to invite him too - but I'm hoping that might be a good thing (as long as he can actually see where he's blasting, with all the slimed-down hair over his eyes!) Surely he'll have to stop picking on me if I take him to *BLAST YOURSELF BONKERS*?

National
Institute for
Criminal
Enterprises

To: **Dr Alpha Bett, Director**

From: **Operative A**

Date: April 30

Re: Mission "Missile Code Retrieval"

I did not mean to question your authority. But I do wonder why this particular mission needs my very considerable skills. Dear old Mr A. would be turning in his grave to see me, barely recognizable away from a lifetime of glitz and glamour. In a semi-detached house!

Initial assessment of situation:
Security appears minimal at best.
Two targets identified:

Target 1 — man (AKA "Mr Spicer Senior" or "Grandad"), roughly 60s, bearded, wears glasses.
Threat level: low

Target 2 — boy (AKA "Freddy"), 9–10 yrs old, scrawny, blond.
Threat level: mega-low. Super-duper low. So low that there is no official threat level category designed to cover the lowness of this threat.

Operative status list:

Operative A — writer of this assessment and recently moved into position as Lead Operative

Operative B — En route from "Operation Super-Yacht Shark"

Operative C — Missing (see "Operation Super-Yacht Shark")

Operative D — Undercover Operative (in position but strictly not to be contacted directly unless in extreme emergency)

Operative E — aka "the professional" — on standby if required

Awaiting further instructions

National

Institute for

Criminal

Enterprises

To: All Operatives on Mission **"Missile Code Retrieval"**

From: **Dr Alpha Bett, NICE Director and the world's greatest Criminal Mastermind**

(Dictated to and typed by Hafta Killenbury,

Personal Assistant to Dr Alpha Bett)

Date: May 1

Primary objective: obtain Missile Codes — known to be in possession of Agents Bubble and Squeak

This is my brilliant and cunning plan:

Now that rumours are circulating about my reappearance, the world's "top agents" — Agents Bubble and Squeak — will be on my tail.

They will think they are chasing me — but they won't know that I am really luring them with my, erm, brilliance and cunning.

We know they are in possession of the Missile Codes. I will bide my time, send them on a merry dance and then POW! get the Missile Codes from them.

And if they don't give them over easily…

Targets 1 and 2 will come in very handy to help _PERSUADE_ THEM!!!

Operative A: you must gain the trust of Target 1 and 2 and be ready to strike if needed. The other Operatives are to be called on to provide further support. In order to protect intelligence sources and maintain absolute secrecy, proceed with extreme caution.

I want the Missile Codes in my possession in time for the **World Leaders' Summit in Jakarta on July 19.** There, I will use the Missile Codes to hold all the major world leaders to ransom and TAKE OVER THE WORLD.

On July 19, the world's greatest

Criminal Mastermind (ME!) will become the greatest and only leader of the entire world — ha ha ha ha ha!!

WE HAVE 80 DAYS TO COMPLETE OUR MISSION

Oh, and bear in mind...

Remember, the targets identified at 61 Bond Lane may have been assessed as low threat but they are the **direct relatives of Agents Bubble and Squeak,** the most deadly espionage experts working anywhere in the world. Do not underestimate them.

Actually, forget that — it's an old man and a young boy! They can't possibly pose a threat to my awesome plan for world domination. I am, after all, the world's greatest criminal mastermind!

WORST FEARS CONFIRMED! DR ALPHA BETT AT LARGE!

Dr Alpha Bett was forced out of hiding today. The recent rumours and suspected sightings were seemingly confirmed when Dr Bett, the self-styled "World's Greatest Criminal Mastermind", escaped from a gold mine in Tanzania.

Caught on video, later posted online, Dr Bett can be seen emerging from the mouth of the mine, much to the surprise of the miners. Surrounded by dirt and heavy machinery, the notorious Dr Bett cut an intriguing figure, dressed all in white, with his signature A-Z gold chains. Two people were hot on his tail but Dr Bett was wearing something on his back that turned out to be a jetpack. He calmly flew up and away, leaving the unidentified pursuers to scramble around, trying to make chase using a digger. The online footage is grainy, so it is impossible to tell the identities of Dr Bett's chasers, although close inspection of the video leads us to believe that it was a man and a woman (one of whom appeared to be on the phone at the time), probably with connections to the International Espionage Agency. The IEA was unavailable for comment.

Mr and Mrs Spicer
The International Federation of Sprout Farmers
11353
Outer Castonga

May 5

Dear Mum and Dad,

Thank you for your phone call but it was really difficult
to hear what you were saying - the phone line was even
noisier than normal. I could hear someone shouting about
digging and you were very out of
breath - I didn't know digging for
sprouts was such noisy, physical work!

I _did_ manage to hear what you said about my
birthday, though...

WHAT DO YOU MEAN YOU WON'T MAKE IT HOME?

You <u>said</u> this year would be different. You PROMISED you'd take me to the *BLAST YOURSELF BONKERS* laser game. I'd told all my new friends. Lamont has stopped his silly joke pranks and even Jordan Fishwick had started being nice to me BECAUSE OF MY PARTY. Now what am I going to do?

There's still SO LONG to go. Maybe your work in **OUTER CASTONGA** will finish sooner than you expect? Really – how hard is it to grow sprouts? I wish you didn't have to work away at all. If you came back, I wouldn't have to write these letters and we could all hang out like a normal family. Wouldn't that be fab? AND you could take me to *BLAST YOURSELF BONKERS*. Please come back for my birthday. I will only turn ten once.

SUPER PLEEEEAAAAAASSSSSSE?

Love

Freddy

P.S. Just because my letter will take AGES to get to

you, don't think I won't still be annoyed about my party.

PROTECTION AGENT DESIREE
DELICATA REPORT TO IEA/IFSF
MAY 6

ALL OK HERE. NOTHING UNUSUAL
TO REPORT.

MET FREDDY IN STREET.

HE WAS UPSET ABOUT HIS PARENTS'
SPROUT WORK AND THEM BEING
AWAY.

WE DON'T WANT HIM QUESTIONING
THE COVER STORY - SEND MORE
SPROUTS!

• • •

Mr and Mrs Spicer
The International Federation of Stinky Sprout Farmers
11353
Outer Castonga

May 7

Dear Mum and Dad,

Have you changed your minds? Can you come back for
my party? Maybe you could ask your bosses? Seriously,
do they know how amazing *BLAST YOURSELF BONKERS*
is supposed to be??? If you explain, they would ~~DEFINATELY~~
DEFINITELY understand. Please, please, please, please, please?

Jordan Fishwick hasn't called me {FREDDY SPROUT STINK}
once since hearing about my birthday party. It will be YOUR
fault if we don't go to *BLAST YOURSELF BONKERS* .
And then what will Jordan start to call me?

Are you _sure_ Grandad's the best person to look after me? It's not just all the sprouts he feeds me. ~~I think he's going a bit barmy.~~ He lost his reading glasses yesterday. I know I'm not supposed to go into your study but I'd seen some glasses on your desk that I thought he could borrow. I didn't think you'd mind. He says his eyesight has never been better. He told me he can now see through walls! Does he really think that I'm going to believe him? I am nearly ten! Of course he can't see through walls. He has suddenly got better at hide-and-seek though.

↓ ↓
COME BACK FOR MY BIRTHDAY!
↑ ↑

love

Freddy

COMMS FROM SIR MUSTARD-GR

JOLLY GOOD WORK WITH FREDDY. AGENT DESIREE DELICATA. YOU ARE HANDLING YOUR PROTECTION WORK ADMIRABLY. A HEARTY PAT ON THE BACK FOR YOU. THE SPLENDID INTERNATIONAL FEDERATION OF SPROUT FARMERS COVER STORY REMAINS ROCK SOLID. MORE SPROUTS ARE ON THEIR WAY, AS PER YOUR REQUEST.

NOT WISHING TO INTRUDE FURTHER ON YOUR TIME BUT WOULD YOU MIND TERRIBLY TAKING RESPONSIBILITY FOR POSTING THE LETTERS FREDDY IS WRITING TO HIS PARENTS? WE DID NOT ANTICIPATE FREDDY BEING SUCH A PROLIFIC WRITER. YOU WILL NEED TO DIVERT EACH LETTER TO AGENTS BUBBLE AND SQUEAK'S SPECIFIC LOCATION AT ANY GIVEN TIME. IT IS REALLY QUITE A BORE! BY OFFERING TO POST FREDDY'S LETTERS FOR HIM, YOU WILL CEMENT YOUR POSITION AS TRUSTED ADULT AND HELP US OUT OF THIS STICKY WICKET. YOU ARE A GOOD EGG.

NS (HEAD OF IEA/IFSF) MAY 8

No one, beyond the IEA, has any clue
as to the real identities of Agents
Bubble and Squeak. Not even Freddy
or his grandad know! Absolute top
secrecy is key to the success of
our esteemed organization. And our
top-notch top secrecy means the
location of the missile codes also
remains inordinately well concealed.
Marvellous work all round, not that I
expect any less from the cream of the
International Espionage Agency.

With that rogue, Dr Alpha Bett,
on the loose again, Agents Bubble
and Squeak are our greatest hope.
Clearly, Dr Bett has no clue that our
best agents are on his tail. It is very
satisfying to be one step ahead of the
no-good scallywag!

Keep up the good work. What ho!

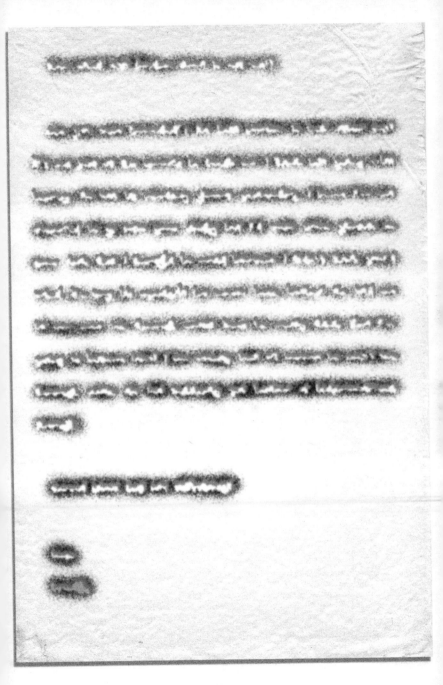

Mr and Mrs Spicer
The International Federation of Sprout Farmers
11353
Sprouter Castonga

May 11

Dear Mum and Dad,

Did you get my last letter? Could you *actually* read it?
I think there was something wrong with the pen I used.
It was from your study. You know - the one with green
ink and the sprout picture on the side?

The ink must have gone off or something.

Because of that stupid pen, I got into trouble at
school. Some homework I did (really carefully - honest)
ended up with holes all through it. Mr Norbert thought

I'd done it as some kind of *joke*. Why would I do homework as a joke? What would be the point? I asked him that <u>but he didn't care</u>. He gave me detention, which was

sooooooo unfair. It wasn't my fault the pen was bad.

If you couldn't read my last letter, you didn't miss much. But I do now have interesting things to tell you about.

1) When I got detention (which I know is a bad thing - blah, blah, blah - please don't have a go at me about that. <u>It wasn't my fault</u>). I was in there with Jordan Fishwick. He was dead impressed to see me in detention. And he's promised to stop taking my Pom-Bears after we go to

BLAST YOURSELF BONKERS .

2) After getting detention, I suggested a brilliant new article to Samira Hadid for **The _Fleming Bulletin_** : "*Do I deserve this? Unfair detentions and unreasonable teachers*". She shook her head ~~so her hair shimmered and sparkled in the light and did that cute little crease thing again above her nose~~ so I guess she didn't like it.

3) Choir is going well. The choir teacher is super pleased that there are now boys in Fleming Voices so she's trying to find new songs for us. When Lamont has to sing really high, his eyebrows almost disappear into his hair! I think the teacher must have noticed that I'm actually a good singer. Lamont told me Miss Davis is wanting me to do a solo verse at the next rehearsal, so I've been practising that loads. ~~Maybe my singing will impress Samira, even if my ideas for magazine articles don't~~

4) Grandad is happy. Him and Mrs Allbright from next door keep chatting over the garden fence and he always gets a bit embarrassed around her. He always takes off his glasses. He said he shouldn't be looking at her drawers but I don't understand why he's bothered about seeing her kitchen cupboards. With Mrs Allbright around, me and Grandad aren't playing as much hide-and-seek now. I miss that. I wonder if there's a World Championship in hide-and-seek? Grandad is so amazing he'd be sure to win it! I mean, he doesn't hide that well, but since using the glasses from your study, he's been able to find me anywhere!

"I'm pleased Grandad's found a friend, but what about me missing my friend? Still nothing from Ajay. I'm sure he's forgotten about me.

I've got my fingers crossed you'll be back for my birthday.

BLAST YOURSELF BONKERS

still has spaces (Grandad rang and checked). My classmates can't wait - NONE of them have been before because it's crazy expensive! I asked Grandad if he'd book it but he said "Not on your Nelly" when he found out how much it is. Seriously - does Grandad EVER spend any money? I don't think I've even seen him with a wallet. What a meany!

Love

Freddy

PS We're out of chocolate milk powder. I've added it to the shopping list in capital letters - MA TEENY'S PREMIUM CHOCOLATE MILK POWDER and I've even drawn a little picture to remind him what the tin looks like - but I am worried what Grandad will *actually* buy.

To: **Operative A** (Lead Operative)

From: **Dr Alpha Bett,** NICE Director

and the world's greatest criminal

mastermind (dictated to and typed by

Hafta Killenbury, PA to Dr Alpha Bett)

Date: May 12 (68 days remaining)

Re: Mission "Missile Code Retrieval"

Instruction for Operative A

Take out Target 1.

Repeat: Take out Target 1.

National

Institute for

Criminal

Enterprises

To: **Operative A** (Lead Operative)

From: **Dr Alpha Bett**, NICE Director

and the world's greatest criminal

mastermind (dictated to and typed by

Hafta Killenbury, PA to Dr Alpha Bett)

Date: May 12 AGAIN (68 days remaining

STILL)

Re: Mission "Missile Code Retrieval"

URGENT

**Clarification of instruction for
Operative A**

Take Target 1 (AKA "Mr Spicer Senior",

AKA "Grandad") **OUT ON A DATE.**

Do not "take him out"!! Do not kill.
Repeat. Do not kill.

That was nearly serious!

Miss Killenbury, YOUR mistake meant
I accidentally issued orders to KILL
Target 1. That would have blown the
whole operation.

This is the best opportunity I
have had IN YEARS for achieving
WORLD DOMINATION! Do not ruin it by
giving ambiguous instructions, Hafta
Killenbury!

I need you to take responsibility for
your SERIOUS ERROR, Miss Killenbury.

65

Why are you still typing what I am
saying?

Stop typing!

You don't need to be typing this!
Your services are no longer required,
Hafta Kille

Mr and Mrs Spicer
The International Federation of Sprout Farters
11353
Outer Castonga

May 14

Dear Mum and Dad,

Grandad is going SERIOUSLY loopy. Whenever he's wearing
his glasses, he's spending his time following "invisible wires
and pipes" around the walls in our house. He only stopped
when he got distracted by your favourite painting in the
lounge, Dad. He kept saying, "I can see
a safe. A big, secret safe!" Odd - I can
only see a boring bowl of sprouts! ~~He's
totally off his rocker!~~ Maybe next time
you go away, I could go stay with Aunty
Sam instead?

But the big news is...

Grandad and Mrs Allbright went out <u>on a date!</u> Can you believe it? I knew Grandad liked her coz he seems to go really flustered when she's around. I think he was TOO shy to ask her out though, so, in the end, SHE ASKED HIM!!

Grandad got really nervous and tried to think of somewhere nice and romantic to take Mrs Allbright. When Mrs Allbright turned up, she had even more make-up on than usual, and when I swallowed, I could taste her perfume – YUCK!

Mrs Allbright's perfume, however, does taste better than my new chocolate milk. Grandad ignored my shopping list drawing and instead picked something called "Budget

Boris's Chocolate-flavour Drink." It tastes like a mixture of teachers' tea breath and the school library's carpet.

*Does Not Contain Any Actual Chocolate

LIBRARY CARPET

TEACHER'S TEA BREATH

Anyway, Grandad and Mrs Allbright seemed to have a lovely time but I wish that Grandad had been generous enough to pay for a babysitter. And I ~~definately~~ definitely wish I hadn't had to go out with them! Grandad insisted on ordering for him and Mrs Allbright - which was tricky because Grandad hadn't worn his glasses on the date. ~~I think he thinks he looks better without them, which is just silly!~~ I ordered something called "Rosenkohl". Sounds nice, doesn't it?

It was not. IT WAS SPROUTS!!!!

Thankfully, Grandad wasn't paying any attention to what I was doing so I left the sprouts and just ate seven bread rolls instead. Best. Meal. Ever.

After the date, Grandad walked Mrs Allbright to her door and gave me the keys to let myself in. Guess who I bumped in to as I walked to our front path? Desiree! I almost didn't notice her coz she looked just like one of the rose bushes. She always checks how I'm feeling, which is dead nice - she knows I'm missing you. And she's offered to babysit next time Grandad goes out. That will be better!

Still hoping you'll be back for my birthday. Only ten days to go now!

And today at school, Jordan Fishwick didn't steal my Pom-bears! Once we've been to *BLAST YOURSELF BONKERS*.

maybe we'll even become friends! I told Samira Hadid about going to *BLAST YOURSELF BONKERS*. She said she might - MIGHT - be interested in an article about it. THAT'S SO EXCITING!!!!!! ~~She didn't even get that cute crinkle above her nose as she said that   and she SMILED at me~~

So you HAVE to come back for my birthday.

Love

Freddy

National

Institute for

Criminal

Enterprises

To: **Dr Alpha Bett**, Director

From: **Operative A** (Lead Operative)

Date: May 15 (65 days remaining)

Re: Mission "Missile Code Retrieval"

Is this what I'm reduced to? Having
to take an old man out on a date? A
man who is too much of a skinflint
to pay for a babysitter? There
was a time when the most fabulous
people imaginable were falling over
themselves to take me to incredible
places: St Tropez, Aspen, Casablanca.
How has it come to this? A second-rate
mission with second-rate targets.

National

Institute for

Criminal

Enterprises

To: **Operative A** (Lead Operative)

From: **Dr Alpha Bett**, NICE Director
and the world's greatest criminal
mastermind (dictated to and typed
by Stan Danshoot, new PA to Dr Alpha
Bett)

Date: May 16 (64 days remaining)

Oh boo hoo! My heart bleeds! Can you
hear me playing a tiny violin for you?
Stop complaining! How dare you
complain TO ME! Count yourself lucky
that **you** were selected to be one of
my elite operatives. **You** have the
chance for glory and wealth beyond

your wildest dreams. And all you have to do is babysit a couple of boring civilians? Poor you! I am putting myself in mortal danger, playing cat-and-mouse with _real_ agents.

I don't want to hear another whinging word from you. My genius plan is working and it will all be worth it when you're relaxing on your own private island. Which island would you like? Hawaii? Australia?

If you think you've got troubles, just listen to this:

As if my plan for world domination wasn't enough to contend with, I've now learnt that I've been named as the **only legal guardian** of Operative C's child. With Operative C still missing, apparently I'm supposed to step up and look after the little maggot. If I'd known that "Operation Super-Yacht Shark" was going to cause me so much trouble, I wouldn't have bothered with it. But Operative C did need teaching a lesson. Why do such terrible things happen to me? I mean, who wants to be guardian to a **ten-year-old boy**? What a pain! I'm sure the child is fine in the orphanage for now. I imagine orphanages have come a long way since my time — probably more like five-star hotels these days, with tellies and proper bedding and everything.

Mr Danshoot — add sorting out this annoying guardian issue to my to-do list. Way, way down the list.

You didn't need to type that bit.

Or that bit.

That was a note to you, not to Operative A.

Why are you still typing?

STOP IT!

Mr and Mrs Spicer
The International Federation of Stinky Farters
11353
Outer Castonga

May 17

Dear Mum and Dad,

I wish you could send letters to me again. The phone calls
are rubbish – I can barely hear you. Did you say you're
on your way home? I'm keeping my fingers and toes and
everything else crossed too.

   And if you do manage to get back, then we can go to

BLAST YOURSELF BONKERS   too so that would
be a double-whammy of aceness. Lamont keeps asking me
about it, but I'm not sure how much of a real friend he is.
Apparently he was "only joking" about Miss Davis wanting

me to sing a solo verse in choir. I can't believe I fell for it AGAIN! Imagine how embarrassing it was when I started on my "solo". EVERYONE just _stared_ at me, including Samira Hadid ~~and I couldn't tear my eyes away from the crease above her nose while I sang~~

Grandad and Mrs Allbright have been spending LOADS of time together. When they look at each other sometimes it's like they go all gooey-eyed. If they were cartoon characters, lots of love hearts would fill the sky around them.

Sometimes Mrs Allbright catches me looking at them and she gives me a secret wink. I like her but I'm surprised she has the time, with all the building work she's having done. It's a carpet-fitter van outside her house this week!

But it might be all over with Grandad and Mrs Allbright anyway after tonight. Grandad was supposed to go around to her house for tea but he's fallen asleep instead! Grandad was making lots of effort to look all smarty-fancy this time so was wearing a suit! (I think it was an old suit because it smelt like the back of the wardrobe - but that's maybe better than smelling of SPROUTS). He didn't have any cufflinks for his shirt but LUCKILY I'd seen some on the desk in your study so didn't think you'd mind if he borrowed them. I was helping him put the first cuff link in his shirt cuff when there was this sharp POP followed by a long HISS. Had Grandad just let out some of his spout wind while standing right next to me?!!

"Urgh. Grandad. That's disgusting." I said.

Grandad then said he was feeling funny and, next thing I knew, Grandad sat on his bed and fell asleep. He's *still* sleeping. ~~He's snoring away upstairs as I write this.~~

Thankfully, Desiree had offered to come over while Grandad was on his date, so I didn't spend the evening alone. I showed her Grandad asleep on his bed - Desiree checked him over and said there was "nothing to worry about". It's good to have her around. I told her all about how I'm missing you and how I've been writing you all these letters and - guess what? - Desiree immediately offered to help post them for me to make sure they get where they need to be. She said I don't even need to worry.

about paying for stamps any more!

   Desiree is so kind - it's like she always knows what to say to make me feel better. I told her I am worried you won't make it back for my party. She said that your sprout work must be super important to take you both away for so long and I have to try hard to understand. She said she was sure you'd be trying your best to "complete your mission" and come back to me. Isn't that a strange way of describing your job?! But SPRUTS can be a mission, I guess! Ha ha - complete your "sprout mission" and come back for my birthday.

love

freddy

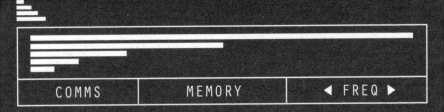

PROTECTION AGENT DESIREE
DELICATA REPORT TO IEA/IFSF
MAY 17

AS REQUESTED, I WILL BE POSTING
FREDDY'S LETTERS FROM NOW ON.

THERE WAS A SLIGHT SNAFU WITH
GRANDAD, FREDDY AND SOME IFSF-
ISSUE CUFF LINKS.

NOTHING TO WORRY ABOUT. I HAVE
EVERYTHING UNDER CONTROL.
IN ORDER TO ENSURE SUSPICIONS
ARE NOT AROUSED, SEND MORE
SPROUTS.

PANDA-MONIUM AT UENO ZOO! DR ALPHA BETT ON THE RUN!

The usual crowds of tourists at Ueno Zoo, Tokyo, got more than they bargained for today, in what turned out to be the latest chapter in the Dr Alpha Bett story.

Eyewitnesses began to report strange behaviour by two of the giant pandas soon after the zoo opened. At midday precisely, without warning, the two suspect "pandas" climbed over the enclosure fence and ran to the Five-Storied Pagoda, causing mass panic. In the mayhem, only a handful of visitors witnessed the real action of the day: Dr Alpha Bett appeared from the Pagoda, which he had apparently been using as his latest lair! On seeing the "pandas" approach, Dr Bett calmly climbed into a small submersible in the Pagoda's moat and disappeared. Extensive searches of Ueno Zoo's grounds have recovered nothing except for two very realistic panda suits (one in a men's large and one in a women's medium). DNA from human hairs found in the suits could not be matched with anyone on any database – is this proof of involvement by the International Espionage Agency? The IEA remains unavailable for comment.

Hi Freddy

Just a quick note to say we're thinking of you and missing you. It's been a while since we received any letters from you, but do keep writing them and we'll get them soon! We hope Grandad is ponda pondering to your needs and that Desiree is also proving to be helpful. We're so sorry we can't make it back for your birthday. We are still trying! But if we can't, we will make it up to you.

Love and Hugs
Mummy and Daddy

Freddy Spicer
61 Bond Lane
Fleming
Flemingshire
BR0 CA1

Pandas Chi-Chi and Michael enjoying the spring blossom in Ueno Zoo, Tokyo

ARGH! Stupid pen!

I was writing you a quick letter in your study coz I was just putting the cufflinks back on your desk when I saw...

IS IT????

CAN IT BE...???

The new

Brain Blaster 3000?

from the shape and size, I THINK SO!!!!!!!!

Of course I will wait for my birthday, but THANKS!!!
You're the best (almost).

You'd be fully the best if you came back here to give it to me yourselves. And to take me and my mates to *BLAST YOURSELF BONKERS*!

In other ~~good~~ news, Grandad finally woke up yesterday. Don't old people sleep for a long time? He says he feels great ~~but he's still sure he can see through walls~~. He never takes the new glasses off except when he's with Mrs Allbright.

I was worried Mrs Allbright wouldn't forgive Grandad for missing their date, so when she came round I told her about Grandad's sprout wind and then falling asleep. I think it helped. They're now slurping sprout soup together. It's disgusting. But probably quite sweet if you're an old person.

Hoping you're on your way back RIGHT NOW. I can't wait to be BLASTING MYSELF BONKERS!!! Oh, and to see you both, of course.

love

Freddy

P.S. My shoes have started to hurt. I'll need new ones when you're back.

P.P.S. Please don't buy me them as a lame birthday present.

Mr and Mrs Spicer
The Stinkernational Federation of Stupid Sprout Farmers
11353
Outer Piggin' Castonga

May 22

Dear Mum and Dad.

I'M REALLY ANGRY WITH YOU!!!!!!!

BAD NEWS - *BLAST YOURSELF BONKERS*

is fully booked for my birthday. So even if you get home.

my party is already ruined. IT'S THE WORST THING EVER!!!!!

AND I won't get to write that article for

The Fleming Bulletin

At least I _think_ you've bought me the Brain Blaster

3000. Grandad has said we can have a blaster and water gun party in the garden – because it won't cost anything. It'll have to do. Mrs Allbright is going to bake me a cake.

Two days to go to my birthday. You _can_ still keep your promise to be home, at least!!

Love

Freddy

P.S I had to tell all my friends about the party. Jordan ate my WHOLE lunch as revenge. Except for the sprouts.

P.P.S Can you tell Grandad to stop putting sprouts in my packed lunch? Even if he disguises them in a frittata, I KNOW THEY'RE IN THERE!

TWIST & SPROUT

It's YOUR BIRTHDAY!

To Our Special Freddykins

Happy 10th Birthday

Lots of Love and Hugs
Mummy and Daddy

P.S. Still no letters from you
for a while. Have you stopped
sending them? Please write soon.

XXXXX

Mr and Mrs Spicer
The Interfartional Farteration of Stink Farters
11353
Outer Castonga

May 24

Dear Mum and Dad,

OH MY GOODNESS!

Thank you. Thank you. Thank you.

THE BLASTER IS AMAZING!!!!!!!!!!!!!!!!!!!!!!!!

Where did you get it? It's not a Brain Blaster 3000 but

it's EVEN BETTER!

At first Lamont insisted the blaster wasn't a real blaster. But then we tested it on a plant pot and it exploded into a million pieces! I think Lamont was just jealous. And, after the choir solo incident, does he really think I'll going to fall for his "jokes"? I am now ten, after all.

My blaster blasted through EVERYTHING!

It was like:

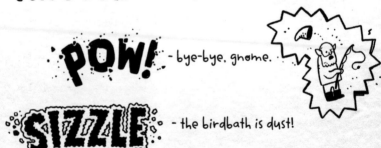

WHOOSH! - there goes the strawberry bushes.

POW! - bye-bye, gnome.

SIZZLE - the birdbath is dust!

We also blasted loads of party food.
Did you know that lemonade tastes
EVEN BETTER when it is blasted? It goes
all hot and sticky! The three jugs full of

Budget Boris's Chocolate-flavour drink, however, was not
any better when blasted (it was worth a try) so we've had
to pour all of it down the drain. Grandad said he's never
seen a drain come up so shiny!

We had loads of fun making our own
popcorn. Maya Peterson did really well at
blasting individual corn kernels at three
metres away. We thought this was the
record BUT THEN Mrs Allbright, from outside our back door
WAY DOWN the whole length of our garden, blasted the
hat off Grandad's favourite gnome! I asked Mrs Allbright
how she managed to do that and she said it was "beginner's

luck". Wow! I wish I'd had the same luck. My shots were nowhere near as accurate – I tried to use the blaster to toast some marshmallows that Lamont was holding up but that did not go well.

Jordan Fishwick turned up to the party, even though he said he wasn't going to coz it wasn't at *BLAST YOURSELF BONKERS*. He brought his camera with him so he'd only come to try and push someone over for a new viral video. Unfortunately, Mrs Allbright must not have seen him and she blasted right at him. Jordan's camera took a direct hit! It is SUCH a good job Mrs Allbright hit the camera and not

Jordan himself – my blaster is REALLY powerful – so Jordan's camera is now just a melted ball of plastic! Mrs Allbright's "beginner's luck" must be super strong!

After Jordan's camera exploded, we just blasted other things in the garden. It's OK – Grandad said we could.

We might need a new shed. It took some serious blasting. The roof disintegrated and the whole shed now creaks and wobbles. And you can kind of see through it. Don't worry – no one's touched your special gardening equipment. We also accidentally blasted a lot of holes in Mrs Allbright's fence. I thought she would get really angry like any grown-up – but she was surprisingly OK about it. And when the blaster beam got too close to her, she did this UNBELIEVABLE jump dive into a commando roll. It was like watching Wonder Woman (if Wonder Woman wore really tight leopard-skin print dresses with fur trims)! Mrs Allbright has many talents. Even the cake she made was awesome because it WASN'T SPROUT-FLAVOURED!!

I had invited Desiree to the party, but she didn't stay for long. I thought Desiree could be a nice friend for Mrs Allbright as she's been so kind to me and Mrs Allbright is also new in the area. BUT when Desiree turned up, I saw Mrs Allbright give her this massive scowl. Desiree left soon after that. I wonder why Mrs Allbright didn't want Desiree there? Oh – I bet Mrs Allbright wants Grandad all to herself and saw Desiree as a rival. Old women are so funny!

Mrs Allbright certainly made sure Grandad had a good time. She brought round something "for the adults" to drink and he got quite tipsy. I heard Grandad talking about holidays. He was going on and on about passports: passports with photos, passports without photos, numbers in passports. It was all really boring but Mrs Allbright was looking at

Grandad like he was saying the most _interesting_ thing anyone has ever said in the history of _speaking_. She must _really_ like him. And if he's talking about going on holiday with her, things must be getting serious!

Thanks so much for the present. I do wonder why a toy blaster is so mega powerful - not that I'm complaining. It's the BEST THING EVER and it almost makes up for you not coming back. And thanks for your card. It's nearly been a week since your last phone call, though. How is sprout farming? Please try to call again soon.

love

Freddy

P.S. Mrs Riley wants to talk to you about when Lamont's eyebrows might grow back.

National

Institute for

Criminal

Enterprises

To: **Dr Alpha Bett**, Director

From: **Operative A** (Lead Operative)

Date: May 25 (55 days remaining)

Mission: Missile Code Retrieval

I have new intelligence of VITAL
IMPORTANCE! No wonder you needed
someone of my calibre on this mission
— you would be lost without me.
Target 1 described to me AT LENGTH a
passport he has seen, which contains
lots of numbers but no photograph —
this has to be the Missile Codes!! I
can't believe that the International
Espionage Agency are STILL hiding

important codes in this old-fashioned way! An important code disguised as a passport? It was popular when I was starting out as an operative, more moons ago than I wish to remember!

But, when you think about it, important codes disguised as passports definitely worked better than some other systems that have been tried over the years. Do you remember the time the old NICE Director decided to hide all the NICE hideout entrance codes in Dexter the Doberman's "Mister Meaty" dog food? It took several days for the codes to be retrieved and even more time to put them back in the correct order! Of course you remember that time! **You** had to sort through Dexter's poop! Ah, good times!

Anyway, from what Target 1 told me, the Missile Code passport is <u>somewhere in the house</u>!

Repeat: The Missile Codes are at 61 Bond Lane.

Target 1 did not divulge their exact location — but, as can be expected from someone of my considerable excellence in the field, I have thought up a clever plan.

Dr Bett — Permission to proceed?

Mr and Mrs Spicer
The International Federation of Sprout Farmers
11353
Sprouter Castonga

May 26

Dear Mum and Dad,

Your phone call last night was SO DIFFICULT to hear. I'm
not sure I heard anything right. I'm sure you were saying
"Don't touch the blaster!" That makes no sense!! Why
wouldn't I want to touch my own birthday present?! Please
try to get a better connection next time. It would be so
much easier if you were here.

Now, I know you said I couldn't go in the shed under
any circumstances because of your special gardening
equipment, but it was about to fall down after ~~getting
blasted at~~ my birthday party. Me, Grandad and Jordan (he

103

came over to ask about borrowing my blaster) have been

sorting it out so there's nothing for you to worry about –

but I do have some questions about the stuff in the shed:

Is this your special gardening equipment?

The other stuff in the shed didn't

look at all like gardening equipment.

Things in the shed:

- a weird rocket-shaped thing that Grandad

says is a sidecar for a motorbike. Grandad is

very excited about it.

- a stash of old fireworks with funny names like

"Military Grade Grenade" and

"Powerful Explosive Device".

What's wrong with Catherine

Wheels?

- a box of wigs and make-up and stuff.

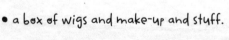

Dead creepy! Grandad said it was probably props from all that amateur theatre stuff you did while we were living in Norfolk.

● an old red telephone (like, really ancient.)
Aren't old phones massive? I don't
know what it was doing in the shed.
Grandad said it that was maybe a
prop too.

The empty shed was too damaged to be saved but we didn't even have to throw it away! Jordan bashed it with a hammer for about two hours (I've never seen him so happy) and then we used my birthday blaster, turned up full. There's no old shed left. Or grass. Or topsoil.

We'd piled everything up inside the house because Grandad is too stingy to buy a new shed – but I kept tripping over the fireworks. _Thankfully._ Mrs Allbright came to the rescue and offered to store everything in her shed. Isn't

she kind!

Love

Freddy

P.S. We didn't think you'd really want to keep that

old red phone so we let Jordan take it home with him to

make up for his melted camera. AND it shut him up about

borrowing my blaster.

National

Institute for

Criminal

Enterprises

To: **Operative A** (Lead Operative)

From: **Dr Alpha Bett**, NICE Director
and the world's greatest criminal
mastermind

(Dictated to and typed by Stan
Danshoot, PA to Dr Alpha Bett)

Date: May 26 (54 days remaining)

Into story-telling now, are you?
Do you think it's funny, retelling
that old story about me, Dexter the
Doberman and unspeakable amounts of
excrement?

Well, let me tell you a story:

There was once a mean old NICE
Director who made a certain *someone*
sift through dog poop for lost codes.
Then that certain *someone* heroically
made the mean old NICE Director get
eaten by Dexter the Doberman. The end.
Remember who is in charge here,
Operative A. Your last communication
was very badly judged.

Don't talk to me about "clever plans".
Your opportunity to act is over. Stand
down, Operative A.

I'm going to send in Operative B to
take a more direct approach and finish
this job.

Mr and Mrs Spicer
The International Federation of Sprout Farmers
11353
Sprouter Castonga

May 27

Dear Mum and Dad,

I'd love to see you both - I wish you were around

right now. I'm not the only person wanting to

see you. Someone called "Blank, John Blank"

popped round yesterday. He said you

**BLANK,
JOHN
BLANK**
were old friends and you met

when you worked in Ustafia.

Did you grow SPR🔘UTS

there too? Do you remember him? Big

(like the size of a door big) and a cool scar

down one side of his face?

I didn't want to seem rude, so I invited Blank, John Blank in and offered him some chocolate milk. I saw he was wearing a gun ~~holder-thingy~~ holster - I think he must be American. I said, "Oh, if you like guns, you should see my Amazing Super Birthday Blaster." I got it and I told him about blasting all the things in the garden. I could tell he was impressed! But when I said I really wanted to try shooting at a _live moving target,_ Blank, John Blank went really pale and muttered something about being "late for something" then ran off. He didn't even leave details for how to get in touch. Sorry.

Do you know it's the half-term holiday now? Except for doing lots of maths homework, there's nothing planned and it's going to be rubbish. I don't even have an idea for a magazine article that I could be writing. ~~All I'm going to be doing is sitting around thinking about how I still don't~~

~~have any real friends - if only Ajay was still around. Jordan~~
~~only likes me for my Blaster (and he still scares me, to be~~
~~honest). Lamont's "jokes" are actually quite mean and he~~
~~just looks silly without eyebrows. Will I be starting back at~~
~~school without a proper friend again? If we'd gone to "Blast~~
~~Yourself Bonkers", things would be different.~~

You know what would make half term AWESOME?
You coming home! (And maybe even still taking me to

BLAST YOURSELF BONKERS

- I'd be totally OK with it as a belated birthday treat!)

Love

Freddy

To: **All remaining Operatives on Mission "Missile Code Retrieval"**

From: **Dr Alpha Bett**, NICE Director and the world's greatest criminal mastermind (Dictated to and typed by Stan Danshoot, PA to Dr Alpha Bett)

Date: May 28 (52 days remaining)

Operative B has resigned with immediate effect, following his meeting with Target 2. I have never seen an operative so shaken by an encounter with a target. He used the words "cold-blooded","callous" and "pant-wettingly terrifying".

Can you believe this? Our most reliably violent operative? He has been sent for counselling.

From what Operative B reported, perhaps we have underestimated Targets 1 and 2? Maybe caution is still needed.

Operative A: You have my permission to proceed with your "clever" plan. Remember, it was thanks to **my brilliance and cunning** that the information about the missile codes came to light.

Lead this area of the mission and use your relationship to gain further access. I am going to continue playing cat and mouse with Agents Bubble and Squeak — we do not want them to return

home. So my work is **just as vital** as
yours. Probably more vital, actually.
Definitely the most important thing
anyone could be doing right now.

Anyway, gain as much access as possible
— by any means necessary — without
making Targets 1 or 2 suspicious.

My AWESOME scheme for WORLD DOMINATION
now entirely depends on your plan,
Operative A. **DO NOT LET ME DOWN!**

William Wilberforce, Hull's most famous MP after John Prescott

Mr and Mrs Spicer
The International Federation of Sprout Farmers
11353
Sprouter Castonga

May 30

Dear Mum and Dad,

Sorry about the postcard I sent yesterday - I realized
only after I'd posted it that I'd written it with that
STUPID SPROUT PEN . I can't believe I
managed to pick up that stupid, defective pen to bring on
holiday!

That's right - I'm on holiday!!

After Mrs Allbright was so helpful about the shed,
Grandad decided to do something nice for her. So we're on

a "mini-break" in Hull! It's very exciting. I've never been on a mini-break before. Do people always travel on coaches for mini-breaks? I know I'm not the only one who was excited to hear about it - Mrs Allbright had ACTUAL REAL TEARS in her eyes as Grandad told her what he'd booked.

We've had a great time and have explored the city lots. We went to this big aquarium called "The Deep" and the *strangest* thing happened... When looking through a porthole, I could have sworn I'd seen Desiree swimming in the tank, wearing a floral scuba suit - but when I ran

round to check, all I could see was
a flounder and a couple of haddock.
What a coincidence that would have
been!

I'll be sad to leave tomorrow - I have my own room in
the bed and breakfast and everything - but the good thing
about the really long coach journey home is that I'll have
plenty time to do my Magical Monster Maths homework.

love

Freddy

National

Institute for

Criminal

Enterprises

To: **Dr Alpha Bett,** Director

From: **Operative A** (Lead Operative)

Date: May 31 (50 days remaining)

Mission: Missile Code Retrieval

Plan progressing well. Targets 1 and 2 suspect nothing.

Keep Agents Bubble and Squeak busy — we do not want them returning home at this crucial time.

Breakthrough expected imminently.

But HULL!

WHY HULL??

Why not Paris?

Or Monaco?

Or Vienna?

Mr and Mrs Spicer
The International Federation of Sprout Farmers
11353
Sprouter Castonga

June 1

Dear Mum and Dad,

You're not going to believe this...

Wait for it...

Grandad and Mrs Allbright

are ENGAGED!!!!!!!!!!!!!!!!!

BLEEEUUUURRRGGGGHHHH!!!

I mean, I like her and

everything, but YUCK! I'm going to get a step-granny! Mrs

A has been acting all giggly and flicking her hair like Freya

Jones does in the lunch queue. I blame Hull. At least it's been

back to school today, so I could escape from the lurve-nest!

121

My toes poked through my shoes this morning. We did not have time to buy any new ones before school, so all I could do was look for some in the house. Good job I'm now the same shoe size as you, Mum, so I'm wearing your black Doc Martins. They fit but the right one is really lumpy under my toe. Maybe we don't need to go shopping for new shoes quite yet coz I actually like how these Docs look.

Grandad's said that I can invite a friend to the wedding, ~~which is a bit tricky, thanks to not really having friends~~. I was thinking about asking Jordan Fishwick but I'm not sure I really want to be his friend now. He makes up some really ~~wierd weird~~ odd stuff. Like yesterday he said that <u>for all of the LAST WEEK, the red phone I gave him has kept flashing and ringing in the middle of the night</u>. He says he tried to make a joke call on it and that has set something off. He says when he answers it, a voice says, "WHAT IS YOUR

POSITION, AGENT BUBBLE AND AGENT SQUEAK? ARE YOU
REQUIRING ASSISTANCE? REMEMBER - KEEP THE MISSILE
CODE SAFE AT ALL COSTS!" How ridiculous. Does he _seriously_
think I'm going to believe him?

And Lamont Riley is really angry about what happened
to his eyebrows at my party. Well, I _think_ he's angry -
actually it is difficult to tell looking at him, without the
eyebrows. It _probably_ didn't help that I told him so. It was
also _probably_ a mistake to let me try to draw some on
with permanent marker. My attempt did
not go well - Lamont looks confused,
delighted and sleepy all at the same
time. Anyway, he's no longer talking
to me, which is making our Magical
Monster Maths pair work really tricky to do.

123

It's been a really bad start to the new half term, to be honest. At least I bumped into Desiree on the way home and she helped me feel better. As soon as this letter is finished, I'm going to drop it round to her house so she can post it for me.

Love

Freddy

PROTECTION AGENT DESIREE
DELICATA REPORT TO IEA/IFSF
JUNE 2

BUBBLE AND SQUEAK EMERGENCY
PHONE ACTIVATED BY ACCIDENT.
NOTHING TO WORRY ABOUT.
HAVE FOUND NEW WAY TO KEEP AN
EYE ON FREDDY.
ALL FINE. I HAVE EVERYTHING
UNDER CONTROL.
I HAVE EVEN PERSUADED FREDDY TO
STOP WRITING SO MANY LETTERS TO
HIS PARENTS. HE'S WRITING *HARDLY
ANY* LETTERS NOW.
SEND MORE SPROUTS FOR GOOD
MEASURE.

Mr and Mrs Spicer
The International Federation of Sprout Farmers
11353
Sprouter Castonga

June 4

Dear Mum and Dad,

Did you know, Mum - your Doc Martins had a <u>camera</u> in the toe?!!!! CRIKEY!!

I kept wearing your shoes and I was like, "These are so uncomfortable," so I did some prodding and prising and CLICK - out popped a camera! THAT'S SO COOL!!

No wonder Docs are so popular!

I told Lamont Riley about it and he's going to check his Doc Martins when he gets home tonight.

NOW FOR THE BIG NEWS...

The wedding is going to be on July 18!! That's, like, ~~seven~~ six weeks away! Apparently, Mrs Allbright wanted it to be EVEN SOONER. I guess, at her age, she doesn't want to wait around too long! But July 18 was the first available date for the wedding venue Grandad's picked (he won't tell me where he's booked - I hope he's picked somewhere glamorous that Mrs Allbright will like). You HAVE to make it back for that FOR DEFINITE. Grandad really wants you there. And I'm going to be best man!

I feel sorry for Mrs Allbright. I don't think she has any friends round here except for me and Grandad. Last night, I looked out of my bedroom window really late and saw Mrs Allbright climbing in to the kitchen renovation van that's

been parked outside her house this week. The van

 flashed its headlights loads of times and then – guess what? – <u>Desiree</u> down the street flashed a torch on and off. It was dark but I could tell it was Desiree because the flashing torch kept lighting up her favourite poppy dress. Mrs Allbright and Desiree did this for ages and then Mrs Allbright climbed out of the van and went back inside. It made me hope they could become friends but when I asked Mrs Allbright about the flashing lights today, she said Desiree just wanted to get a quote for a new kitchen. And no wonder Mrs Allbright didn't invite her into the house last night – it really was *super* late.

But if Mrs Allbright doesn't have friends around, I don't know how she will get ready for the wedding. Grandad has me. Maybe I can help Mrs Allbright too? The most important thing is that she doesn't turn into a BRIDEZILLA like you said Mum did at your wedding, Dad. Ha Ha! Do you remember, Dad? You said about Mum turning into a Bridezilla and I asked if that was something like this (all green and scaly) ...

and you said "NO - A BRIDEZILLA IS FAR MORE TERRIFYING!!" Please try to get back for the wedding.

Love

Freddy

WHAT A SHOW! LATEST DR BETT SIGHTING AT SYDNEY OPERA HOUSE

Visitors to the world-famous Sydney Opera House witnessed real-life drama today, as the landmark became the latest setting for the ongoing pursuit of Dr Alpha Bett, the world's greatest criminal mastermind.

As tourists queued to visit the iconic 1970s building in Sydney Harbour, Dr Alpha Bett, dressed all in white and wearing his signature A-Z gold chains, could be seen standing calmly on one of the Opera House's many roofs. Two unidentified people were seen using climbing gear to scale the side of the building. Before they reached Dr Bett, however,

the self-styled Criminal Mastermind used a crossbow to shoot a bolt connected to a wire at a boat waiting on the harbour. He then zip-wired down to the boat, severed the wire and sailed away, leaving the climbers in his wake.

It is the belief of this paper that the two people in pursuit of Dr Bett are the suspected International Espionage Agents who have been observed at the previous locations at which Dr Bett has surfaced. The International Espionage Agency was unavailable for comment.

~~G'day~~ Hello!

I hope we're not missing too much while we're away. ~~Sprouts~~ are proving far more difficult to _catch_ grow than anyone first thought. It's an uphill struggle — climbing, striving and chasing, only to have glory sail away from us at the last second. It's frustrating and hard work but it will be worth it once we're done. Still haven't caught up with your latest letters — the Outer Eastongan post service really is terrible — but we're really looking forward to having a good read of them when we do! Make sure you keep writing to us about everything you're doing. We're missing you SO MUCH.

Love and Hugs
Mummy and Daddy

Freddy Spicer
61 Bond Lane
Fleming
Flemingshire
BR0 C£1

Fireworks over Sydney Harbour

131

COMMS FROM SIR MUSTARD-GR

SUCH A BORE, ALL THIS NONSENSE WITH
THE BEASTLY DR ALPHA BETT.

YOU ARE DOING TOP-NOTCH WORK,
PROTECTION AGENT DESIREE. THANK
YOU FOR CLARIFYING THE UNFORTUNATE
ACCIDENTAL ACTIVATION SITUATION WITH
OUR EMERGENCY TELEPHONE AND JOLLY
WELL DONE FOR GETTING FREDDY TO
LIMIT HIS LETTER-WRITING POPPYCOCK.
HE WOULD HAVE BANKRUPTED THE IEA
WITH THE POSTAL COSTS, BY GINGER! A
VIGOROUS HANDSHAKE AND A HEARTY
PAT ON THE BACK FOR YOUR CONTINUED
TOIL.

OUR SUPERLATIVE SPROUT COVER STORY
IS STILL HOLDING AND THE MISSILE
CODES REMAIN HAPPILY HIDDEN. BUT

● ● ●

s (Head of IEA/IFSF) June 5

THIS BOTHERSOME MISSION IS TAKING AGENTS BUBBLE AND SQUEAK FAR LONGER THAN PREDICTED, SO I HAVE AUTHORIZED A SECOND PROTECTION AGENT TO PROVIDE FURTHER SUPPORT.

PROTECTION AGENT BEAN (AKA HARRY COVAIR) WILL BE ARRIVING SHORTLY AND, AS A MASTER OF INTEGRATION, WILL PROVIDE SECURITY FOR FREDDY WITHOUT CAUSING UNDUE ALARM. THIS FIRST-RATE AGENT, VETTED AT THE HIGHEST LEVEL BY AGENTS BUBBLE AND SQUEAK THEMSELVES, WILL BE REPORTING DIRECTLY TO ME. HE'S AN ABSOLUTE BRICK.

MORE SPROUTS BEING DISPATCHED FORTHWITH.

Mr and Mrs Spicer
The Stupid International Federation of Boring Sprout
Farmers
11353
Outer Castonga

June 8

Dear Mum and Dad,

Things are not going well. Lamont Riley's Doc Martins didn't
have a camera in them and his parents are annoyed
that he ripped them apart looking for one. You
might have to buy him some new shoes too.

Lamont is really angry at me - he says it was really
mean for me to play a trick on him. He said he would
never have done anything like that! He told Mr Norbert
in his stupid loud voice about the camera in MY shoes. Mr
Norbert confiscated them off me coz, "*Electronic devices*

aren't allowed at Fleming School." He's said he'll only give them back when he sees one of my parents - so now there's ANOTHER reason for you to get back. And I got detention again. If we ever get to go to BLAST YOURSELF BONKERS, Lamont is officially uninvited.

When the Docs were taken off me, I didn't have any other shoes to wear. I had to look through lost property to find something. It was really smelly and *almost* impossible to find anything that fitted. And there were so many single shoes. How does anyone lose a single shoe? Then something really surprising happened - Desiree turned up! She's just got a job as a dinner lady at school - so she said she'll be able to see me EVEN MORE! She helped me look through all the DISGUSTING lost property and, thankfully, there were some brown velcro sandals that were just

135

about my size, so I wore those home. They weren't great and I didn't even know whether to wear them with or without socks, but at least Grandad has now agreed to go shopping. We're heading out right this second.

love

Freddy

P.S. I have thought of a new article for **Fleming Bulletin**
"*Lost Property: A School Sandal Scandal*". I'll suggest it to Samira tomorrow.

:

P.P.S. Oh, I almost forgot ... EXCITING NEWS... We're getting a new boy starting class tomorrow. The teacher has asked me to show him around. I really hope he will turn out to be a new friend for me. Still no word from Ajay. It's like he never existed.

National

Institute for

Criminal

Enterprises

To: **Operative A** (Lead Operative)

From: **Dr Alpha Bett**, NICE Director
and the world's greatest criminal
mastermind (Dictated to and typed by
Stan Danshoot, PA to Dr Alpha Bett)

Date: June 9 (40 days remaining)

I hope you know what you're doing.
I'm risking everything while you're
playing the **blushing bride to be**.

Thanks to my **amazing plan**, Agents
Bubble and Squeak are still chasing me
all over the globe. I have to trust
you to make this work. Forty days to

go — don't let me down! You wouldn't
want to be fed to Anastacia, my pet
anaconda, would you?

Mr and Mrs Spicer
The International Federation of Sprout Farmers
11353
Outer Castonga

June 10

Dear Mum and Dad,

I'm actually starting to look forward to the wedding. The
most AMAZING thing about it is that Mrs Allbright has
got Grandad to actually SPEND SOME MONEY! Looks like
Grandad does have a wallet after all - ha ha! Grandad's
even promised to buy me a suit. He's said I can just wear
my school shoes he bought me but they are a bit naff - I
wish I had your Docs back, Mum.

The new boy in class is called Harry Covair. Apparently
he's at school for a term as an exchange pupil. I like him

already. When he first walked into class, he threw his hat and coat and they both landed PERFECTLY on the hooks. He's really cool.

Harry is not like other boys in my school. He is much taller than me and his voice is really low and deep. PLUS he already shaves! When do I get to start shaving? You said it wouldn't be FOR AGES.

I have had a great idea to write an article for **The Fleming Bulletin** about being a new boy. using Harry as an example - surely Samira Hadid would love that idea! I snuck into the school office to do some research on Harry's background and on the school form where it says parental occupation it says "Espionage". That must be French for SPINACH!! Wow! We have so much in common!

Grandad will be dead upset if you don't make it back for the wedding. Please try. (˄‿)

love
Freddy

P.S. When Harry's dad collected him in the car after school (the car was SO COOL – it had blacked-out windows), I heard him call his dad "Frank". That's so ~~sofisticated/~~ ~~sofistikated/sophisti...~~ grown up. I'm going to start doing that.

AGENT BEAN REPORT TO IFSF/IEA
JUNE 10

CONTACT HAS BEEN MADE WITH FREDDY
SPICER.

THERE ARE SOME SIGNS OF UNUSUAL
ACTIVITY BUT NOTHING UNDULY
CONCERNING. WILL CONTINUE TO ASSESS
THE SITUATION.

FREDDY HAS BEEN VERY WELCOMING. HE
IS A VERY SWEET BOY BUT HE DOESN'T
SEEM TO HAVE MANY FRIENDS AT
SCHOOL, WHICH IS A SHAME BECAUSE HE
IS HILARIOUS. HE CHATTED TO ME FOR
A LONG TIME TODAY ABOUT SPINACH – I
HAVE NO IDEA WHY!

● ● ●

Mr and Mrs Spicer
The International Federation of Sprout Farmers
11353
Outer Castonga

June 12

Dear Bunny and Sterling (what do you think?? Well grown up, eh?),

I can't believe how quickly Harry and I have become good friends. It's a shame he'll only be at school for the rest of this term – when he leaves I'll be sad again, like when Ajay went. But at least Harry's here now and he's agreed to come to Grandad's wedding. Hopefully you'll meet him.

At the same time, things have got much worse with Jordan – it's like me and him are back to square one. Yesterday, Jordan stole my lunch again coz he said he didn't lie about the phone calls from the big red phone. Then he called me STINK-BREATH SPROUTY-BUM. ~~I was trying not to cry~~ when Harry grabbed Jordan and held him above his head like a body-builder until Jordan started screaming. I even got the Pom-Bears back! I almost felt sorry for Jordan. ALMOST.

And Harry has joined the school choir. Miss Davis is _really_ delighted - she says it's the first time she has had a BASS voice in Fleming Voices and she's dead excited coz it means we can "harmonize properly". Miss Davis thinks we might even stand a chance at the end-of-year Competition of the Choirs. How cool is that? It would be a full day out from school. And a day out that I get to spend ~~staring at~~ with Samira Hadid! I wonder if we could work together to write something about the choir for

The Fleming Bulletin? ✮ ✦

Everything is going OK with the wedding preparations. I think you'll like Mrs Allbright. She's very interested in stuff - she's asked me LOADS of questions about you. The other day I heard a clicking coming from your study, so I tiptoed along the corridor. I was so quiet I was like a tiny mouse wearing slippers. To my surprise, it was Mrs Allbright! I could just see the top of her head over the desk and I kept hearing a *click, click, click*. You should have seen her jump when she saw me standing there!

I didn't realize it, but she told me she was actually *trying to play hide-and-seek with me!* Isn't that nice of her? I told her that if she wanted to play hide-and-seek, the two main rules are:

• to make sure the other person knows you've started a game of hide-and-seek,

and

• to be AS QUIET AS POSSIBLE.

Hopefully my help will make her better at the game, but Grandad is so ace at hide-and-seek, she'll never win no matter how quiet she is.

Are you on your way home?

love

Freddy

WORLD'S GREATEST CRIMINAL MASTERMIND HAS **GRAND** PLANS!

Tourists at the Grand Canyon have reported latest sighting of the notorious Dr Alpha Bett.

Dr Bett was not taking any measures to hide himself as he calmly gazed at the magnificent natural wonder from the Grand Canyon Skywalk, his trademark A-Z gold chains glinting in the Arizona sun. The usually busy tourist site emptied quickly as Dr Bett was recognized. Two people dressed as Skywalk guides started to approach the criminal mastermind, when a helicopter rose up from the depths of the canyon and hovered just above, allowing Dr Bett to be hoisted up with a winch.

Suddenly, one of the Skywalk guides ran and leapt to grasp at the feet of Dr Bett in a brave attempt to capture him. Their colleague, however, appeared to be taking a phone call and did not provide support. Dr Bett got away.

Skywalk HQ has denied that any of their staff were involved in the incident with Dr Bett. This latest sighting comes not even a fortnight since the last one. What is Dr Bett planning? Where will he turn up next? We hope the anonymous duo on his tail catch him soon, so the world can go back to being a safer place!

The International Espionage Agency continues to be unavailable for comment.

ARGH! I've just noticed I've been writing with that ~~sprout~~ pen. Why does that keep happening? I guess I should just throw it away.

I had been writing that it was even more difficult *than normal* to hear your phone call yesterday. Did you say something about a chopper? Is that a machine you use to chop sprouts? It was really noisy! Even though you were shouting, I could barely hear you!

Harry came over after school today so I could introduce him to Grandad. It really cheered me up coz Samira rejected the "new boy at school" article. ~~Why is she so tough to impress?~~ I made us some chocolate-flavour drink but it is *really* gross. Harry tried shaking it up just like you do – then we even stuck it in the blender – but it still managed to be lumpy, thick and watery all at the same time. Grandad's said he won't buy any other kind until the Budget Boris tub is finished. Bleurgh!

We played outside with my birthday blaster. Harry was

AMAZING with it!!!!! Even Grandad enjoyed himself. I bet Harry plays loads of console games coz he's like a super-sniper. He blasted the ~~chicken-thing~~ weathervane on the top of that church three streets away! Now it spins round like a ... like a headless chicken!

Harry even managed to blast a tiny camera-looking thing that was in the trees at the back of Mrs Allbright's garden. I hope she won't mind. It's a shame that pigeon flew across the laser beam. **SIZZLE**

It's nice having Harry around.

After Harry left, I was tidying up the garden and I saw Grandad wheel an old motorbike into Mrs Allbright's shed. He's started tinkering about in there and keeps grinning and talking about his "surprise for the wedding". But I know what he's doing! He's putting together the motorbike he's just bought with the ~~wierd~~ strange sidecar-thing we found in your shed. I can see why this might be cool - but I really can't see how Mrs Allbright will climb into the sidecar in the tight dresses she wears! Poor Mrs Allbright!

Love

Freddy

P.S. I've cleaned my teeth three times tonight and my mouth still tastes really weird. Grandad said we had chicken for dinner, but now I'm not so sure...

"CHICKEN"

National

Institute for

Criminal

Enterprises

To: **Operative A** (Lead Operative)

From: **Dr Alpha Bett**, NICE Director

and the world's greatest criminal

mastermind

(Dictated to and typed by Stan

Danshoot, PA to Dr Alpha Bett)

Date: June 15 (34 days remaining)

Operative A: Are you CERTAIN you'll

complete your mission in time? My

 brilliance has got us this far but I'm

starting to tire of my cat-and-mouse

game with Agents Bubble and Squeak.

You MUST succeed. Don't forget you

have Operative E at your disposal.

Consider <u>more extreme measures, whilst</u>
<u>maintaining absolute secrecy and</u>
<u>proceeding with complete caution.</u>

What?

Stan, what do you mean that's
impossible to achieve?

Why are you questioning my authority?

And why are you still typing?

Stop typing

Stop t

National

Institute for

Criminal

Enterprises

To: **Dr Alpha Bett,** Director

From: **Operative A** (Lead Operative)

Date: June 16 (33 days remaining)

Mission: Missile Code Retrieval

Patience! Patience! In your great
wisdom, you have placed trust in me
and I WILL DELIVER. I did not leave
my life of luxury to fail, you know.
You promised me an island but, by the
time I've finished, I will deserve an
entire continent!

My plan is working. Target 1 is
understandably besotted with me.

I have achieved almost unlimited access of the Targets' house but progress kept being stymied through interruptions by Target 2.

I have been working on developing a relationship with Target 2. He is an interfering inconvenience but I am getting him on side. *No one* is immune to my charms.

I believe Target 2 will now, unwittingly at least, help me locate the missile codes passport.

Keep you hair on, Dr Bett (if you currently have hair — I find it difficult to keep track). When my plan does succeed, you will have the codes and no one will realize until it is too late!

REQUEST: Please deliver SPECIAL SERUM
#7734 to 63 Bond Lane, Fleming,
Flemingshire ASAP

Mr and Mrs Spicer
The International Federation of Sprout Farmers
11353
Outer Castonga

June 21

Dear Bunny and Sterling,

Mrs Allbright is fantastic. She knew I was spending loads
of time revising for the end-of-year tests this week, so
she really cheered up my dull weekend of revision by
playing hide-and-seek. And I think she's getting better
at it. Good for her! (I just wish I was getting better
at maths - hopefully I won't TOTALLY fail the test but
MAGICAL MONSTER MATHS
has not worked any magic!) This time, I found Mrs Allbright
upstairs in your bedroom and she was being so quiet. I
didn't realize anyone was in the house! She still didn't hear

me coming, though. So when I jumped out, she was so surprised, she nearly had a heart attack! Mrs Allbright then said she's actually planning something SECRET for the wedding and needs me to be her *special wedding helper*!!!

I'm so pleased she's asked me - hopefully this means she won't become mean and grumpy like Mum did before your wedding - and I was about to agree to help but then I had a BRAINWAVE...

I said I'd be her *special wedding helper* IF she promised to take me and my friends to *BLAST YOURSELF BONKERS* after the wedding.

AMAZINGLY, Mrs Allbright has agreed - so as long as I do

a good job of helping and the wedding goes smoothly.

BLAST YOURSELF BONKERS is BACK ON!

I can't wait to tell my friends – and now Harry can come too! Hopefully I can still get an article in **The Fleming Bulletin** by the end of the year! I must tell Samira!

🌀

BLAST YOURSELF BONKERS is my only hope for an article in **The Fleming Bulletin**. Samira Hadid has hated all my other ideas. I even asked her if I could be an "official reporter" at sports day this Friday, but she said no ~~and shook her luscious hair~~. However, as head girl she's also responsible for organizing refreshments for sports day and she has said I can help out with those. I'm going to do the BEST REFRESHMENTS EVER – if I impress Samira, she might be kinder about my article suggestions ~~and she might smile at me again~~. So, even though sports

day would normally be WORSE than tests, I'm actually

looking forward to it. And I've been picked to run the three-legged race with Harry - so I'm in with a chance of WINNING SOMETHING AT LAST - yay!

Love

Freddy

P.S. Having tea at Mrs Allbright's tomorrow ON MY OWN! Apparently she wants to get to know me better. That's really sweet! I asked her if she has a tin of Ma Teeny's Premium Chocolate Milk Powder but sadly not. She did say she was getting something special in for me, though.

Mr and Mrs Spicer
The International Federation of Sprout Farmers that
my mum and dad seem to love more than me.
11353
Outer Castonga, which is very, very, very far away

June 22

Dear Bunny and Sterling,

I've just had tea at Mrs Allbright's house. I don't know why

Grandad was worried about seeing her kitchen drawers -

they're nothing special.

   We just ate sandwiches but she gave me this AMAZING

green drink that seemed to FIZZ,
FROTH
AND BUBBLE

161

whenever I tipped the glass. It tasted really ~~wired/wierd~~ strange but I liked it and asked for more. That made Mrs Allbright very happy and she said I should drink it all up. I asked her what was in the drink but she said it was a "family secret". Maybe when she's married to Grandad and we are officially family, she'll tell me.

After drinking so much of it, I felt queasy. I kept doing strange little burps that made my head spin. And my ears felt like they were hearing everything through water. I think I heard Mrs Allbright say, "Oh good, it's starting to work."

But it really sounded like, "Oooooooooooooooooohhhhhh ggggoooooooooooooooooddddd. IIIIIttttt'sssssssssssssssssss ssstttttaaaaaaaaaaaarrrrrrtttttiihhhhgggg tttooooooooooo wwwwwwwooooorrrrrrrkkkkkk."

She sounded really funny, like she was running out of batteries!

Suddenly, Mrs Allbright flicked on a super-bright lamp and pointed it at me. It made me really squint but it did make all the sounds go back to normal. Better than normal, in fact. It was like I was super-aware of EVERYTHING. I swear I could even hear Grandad working on the motorbike-sidecar thing down the bottom of the garden!

Mrs Allbright said we were going to play a game. I don't know the name of the game, but she asked me LOADS of questions and said I had to try to be AS TRUTHFUL as possible. She asked me what my most embarrassing secret was.

I'd never told anyone - and I didn't really want to tell Mrs Allbright - but my mouth wouldn't stop talking. I suddenly COULD NOT STOP telling the truth!!! ~~I told her all about the time when I pooed in the plant pot outside the back door and then blamed it on next door's dog, Fido. Oh dear, I wasn't supposed to write that here either!!!~~

She then asked me what I knew about your work. I talked for a long time about sprouts and how much I hate them. On and on and on I went. I do really hate sprouts. But then I think she got bored. She started tapping her fingers. She looked like she was chewing a wasp. I told her that. She did not look any happier.

She asked me if I knew anything about codes. I told her about the Code of Conduct at Fleming School. You know, where we all have to R-E-S-P-E-C-T each other. I started our school's Code of Conduct rap:

"R is for respect and responsibility.

E is for everyone - including you and me.

S is for safety, coz safety's really dope.

P is for politeness, say "no thank you", don't say "nope".

E is for 'elpfulness, we all can play our part.

C is for consideration, which means please don't..."

... but Mrs Allbright did not let me finish.

I guess she wasn't that interested in codes after all.

Next, she asked me about hiding places in our house. Ha!

I knew she was trying to get better at hide-and-seek.

"You'll never win against Grandad. He can find me

anywhere." I told her. "It's almost like Grandad's new

glasses have given him X-ray vision!"

Mrs Allbright said she wanted to find out about hiding

places around our house for much smaller things. I told her that wasn't the rule for hide-and-seek and then spent a lot of time explaining the hide-and-seek rules in LOTS OF DETAIL. She still won't beat Grandad, though.

FINALLY, she asked me what I thought ABOUT HER! I said that I thought she was marrying Grandad because she was old and lonely like him. I tried not to say that coz I knew it sounded mean, but my mouth just kept going - blah blah blah. I also told her I was worried she might turn into a Bridezilla at the wedding. I explained that I knew that doesn't mean she will look like a green, wrinkly, scaly monster in a wedding dress but that she will become really mean and scary (and that she is already wrinkly anyway). Then I told her that her moustache made me think of my new friend Harry Covair and I asked her if she could teach me how to shave when I was older. At that moment she suddenly realized the time and here I am now at home in bed. I don't even know whether I won our game or not. Will have to ask her tomorrow.

Wow. I've written a lot today. I don't seem able to stop talking or writing. Like I really want to tell you about the time, Mum, that Dad smashed your favourite vase but hid all the pieces behind the sofa and bought me a WHOLE chocolate bar to stop me from telling you. And I love chocolate. It is so much better than sprouts.

Have I told you how much I hate sprouts?

I hate the taste. I hate how they look. I hate how they smell. I hate being called "Stinky Sprouty Bum Bum" and all other meany sprout names. And I hate that they take you all around the world and away from me.

I didn't really mean to write that. Well, I mean it but I don't know why I can't stop myself from writing it. I miss you loads and loads and loads and want my mummy and daddy back. When I finish this letter, I'm going to have a long cry.

Please come home. Why haven't you come home yet?

Night night.

Love

Freddy

P.S. Don't tell Mrs Allbright but I "borrowed" some of her delicious fizzy green drink stuff – everyone will love it at sports day. I'll do the best refreshments ever!!

National

Institute for

Criminal

Enterprises

To: **Dr Alpha Bett**, Director

From: **Operative A** (Lead Operative)

Date: June 23 (26 days remaining)

Mission: Missile Code Retrieval

Are you sure it was Serum #7734 that you sent me?

Despite a hefty dose, Target 2 was unable to provide any answers to my questions regarding the codes and their hiding place, but I'm still certain he holds the key to finding them. He said nothing useful at all and was, in fact, really quite

insulting! I'm feeling a little hurt,
to be honest.

Or have we underestimated Target 2?
Perhaps Agents Bubble and Squeak have
trained Target 2 so well that, even
under interrogation, he doesn't give
up any information.

Could Target 2's cluelessness be
an act? Surely *no one* can be that
idiotic!

Serum #7734 (or whatever it was)
unsuccessful.

Mr and Mrs Spicer
The International Federation of Sprout Farmers
11353
Sprouter Castonga

June 26

Dear ~~Mum and Dad~~ Bunny and Sterling,

This has been a RUBBISH week. I was so pleased you rang

to wish me luck with the end-of-year tests - but it didn't

help in the end. I tried REALLY hard in my maths test but

realized when I got home that I'd taken that STUPID SPROUT

PEN to school and used it in the test. I tried to talk to Mr

Norbert about it but he was too busy with sports day to

"deal with daft boys who play practical jokes in SERIOUS

tests."

    For sports day, Harry won EVERYTHING (almost)! We

were paired up for the three-legged race and WE WON

BY A MILE!!! I'd never won anything before so I was dead excited.

BUT THEN, Mr Norbert said that it didn't count because Harry had basically carried me down the track – so we were DISQUALIFIED!

I was really upset. ~~I was crying so hard that~~ it was very difficult to carry the green fizzy drinks properly. Harry, Lamont, Jordan and Maya grabbed beakers off the tray but I dropped the rest coz I banged into Desiree. ~~I guess, I didn't see her through my tears.~~ Samira Hadid was really annoyed with me (~~the cute crease came back above~~

her nose). I don't think she'll ask me to do anything for her again, which isn't fair. I didn't mean to drop the tray – maybe Desiree should have looked where *she* was going! And the green fizz was hard to clean up. It's made a big patch of grass on the school field turn a luminous yellow!

I told you it has been a rubbish week! Glad it's the weekend.

love

Freddy

Dear Mr Norbert,

I am writing to say sorry for calling you a "stinky-headed nincompoop" at sports day. I do not know what came over me. Mum grounded me for a week when she heard what I'd said.

Please accept my apologies.

Maya Peterson

Dear Mr Norbert,

Sorry for shouting about that you're a "rubbish teacher with awful coffee breath" at sports day. Mum was really embarrassed and is trying to get me to learn to speak more quietly. She made me write lines at home.

Lamont Riley

DEAR MR NORBERt,

DAD SAYS I HAVE to WRItE A LEttER OF APOLOGY to
YOU FOR REFUSING to RUN IN tHE RELAY, SHOUtING
tHAt SPORtS DAY IS "StUPID AND POINtLESS" AND
VOMItING ON YOUR SHOES. tHAt'S Not FAIR. I
DON't tHINK It WAS MY FAULt - I WAS COMING
DOWN WItH tHE FLU OR SOMEtHING. AND SPORtS
DAY IS StUPID AND POINtLESS.

SOZ ANYWAY,
JORDAN FISHWICK

Dear Mr Norbert,
Please accept my humble apologies for the incident that
took place on sports day. I was, of course, only joking
when I told you that I was an international agent, working
undercover to provide protection for one of your pupils!
Clearly, your excellent teaching has got my imagination
working overtime and your inspiring story-writing
guidance has me indulging in flights of fancy. It will not
happen again.

Again, please accept my apologies for what occurred
during sports day and please forget everything you heard
from me.

Yours sincerely,
Harry Covair (a ten-year-old exchange pupil)

Mr and Mrs Spicer
The International Federation of Sprout Farmers
11353
Sprouter Castonga

June 28

Dear Bunny and Sterling,

Not long now till the wedding. I'm supposed to give a

speech. ARGH! Harry Covair has been helping me write it,

which is really nice of him. I do wonder if the teachers

have put Harry in the wrong year group coz he is so

massive. But he struggles with some things in our class

so it's probably good he's not been put in the year above.

Harry's handwriting is sooooo messy, it's like he's never

been taught how to join up and he's always muttering

"why can't we just type?" He's so funny!

Grandad and me went suit shopping yesterday. I'll look super smart as best man. We looked at new shoes too but none were as nice as your Docs, Mum, so Grandad has said he'll help me get them back from school. I have a cunning plan!

Also, talking about plans, Lamont Riley (his eyebrows are almost back to normal, by the way, so I find him much easier to talk to again) told me about his uncle's wedding and that the best man did all these funny tricks on the married couple. Tee hee! I know what I'm going to do. I don't want to spoil the surprise, so I'll just say that it's going to be sprout-tastic!!

Got to go. So much wedding stuff to work on!

Love

Freddy

P.S. Miss Davis has signed up Fleming Voices into the "Competition of the Choirs". The choir is now huge and REALLY good - loads of boys have joined it since Harry started. He seems to make everything cool.

THE WORLD'S GREATEST CYCLE-PATH?

Stage 2 of world's longest cycle race, the Tour de France, came to an abrupt halt today as the cyclists were overtaken on their way down the mountainous route by a figure dressed all in white, signature A-Z gold chains flapping in the breeze. For a few minutes, Dr Alpha Bett, the world's greatest criminal mastermind, was calmly leading the famous cycle race! Quickly, and from out of nowhere, two unidentified people on motorbikes were seen to be making chase. Dr Bett was pursued down the mountain and into a long tunnel where, it is reported, he disappeared. Extensive searches of the area have not uncovered any clues. Despite no official confirmation, this is probably another embarrassing failure by the International Espionage Agency to apprehend Dr Bett. Where will he appear next?

Bonjour Hello Freddy

We're getting closer to finishing our ~~sprout~~ work. At least, we keep thinking we're getting closer, only to lose ~~sprout~~ in a tunnel at the last minute. How can ~~sprout~~ be one step ahead, all the time?

We can't wait to see you and get back to a normal life. We're so sorry to have left you for so long. It's been so long since we received any letters from you, there must be so much that we've missed. Hopefully you're having a lovely quiet time with Grandad and we haven't missed anything too important or interesting.

We'll be back as soon as possible.

Love and Hugs

Mummy and Daddy

Freddy Spicer
61 Bond Lane
Fleming
Flemingshire
BR0 E11

The French Alps in a Snow Storm

180

Mr and Mrs Spicer
The International Federation of Sprout Farmers
11353
Sprouter Castonga

June 30

Dear Bunny and Sterling.

I got the Docs back from school. Yay!

Mr Norbert had said he'd only give the Docs back to a parent so I came up with this BRILLIANT plan, which involved Grandad and the wigs and make-up that were stashed in your shed. I thought Grandad could pretend to be you. Dad. and ask for the Docs back. As the Docs have been locked away in Mr Norbert's desk. I couldn't see another way to get them back in time for the wedding.

Anyway. Harry said that was too complicated and he

told us to meet him after tea, outside the school gates, with a paperclip, a candle and washing-up sponge. I didn't know what Grandad would think of this plan but he was totally up for an adventure – he said it reminded him of being a "carefree whippersnapper", whatever that is. When we turned up, Harry was there all dressed in black and he even had full camouflage paint on his face, which was probably a bit much.

Harry jumped over the school fence (then he had to jump back to help me and Grandad get over). We checked for cameras and then tried to copy Harry's rolls over the playground – they were just like Mrs Allbright's commando rolls from my party! When we got to outside our classroom window, Harry took the paperclip, sponge and candle and told me and Grandad to keep look-out as he slid the window open and climbed in.

As I was looking around, I saw something blotchy moving about in the shadows. I was glad Grandad was with me coz I started to get a bit scared, but then realized it was just Desiree out on a walk. Her flowery dress matched the ~~roada rodo rhoder roadadend~~ flower bushes outside school so perfectly, I nearly missed her! It's so nice having her around. She must love her job as dinner lady, if she's hanging around Fleming School at night too. And then, only seconds later, Harry reappeared with the Docs! He's AMAZING!!!

So I'm now all sorted for the wedding – and Grandad is delighted he didn't need to spend extra money on new shoes. I can concentrate on helping Grandad and Mrs

Allbright - and then that trip to *BLAST YOURSELF BONKERS*

is as good as mine!!

love

Freddy

P.S. I have NO IDEA how Harry got into a locked desk

with a paperclip, candle and sponge. I noticed there was a

locked drawer in your study desk so I have been trying

to work it out. IT IS IMPOSSIBLE! But when you get home,

you might notice, in that drawer, some bits of sponge and

candle wax that weren't there before - sorry.

Agent Bean report to IFSF/IEA
June 30

I have gained the trust of Freddy
and his grandfather. I am glad to be
helping them while Freddy's parents
are away.

While on an important mission with
Freddy, I noticed Desiree working
surveillance. This had not been
ordered and seemed out of place.
Is Desiree receiving instructions of
which I am unaware?

National

Institute for

Criminal

Enterprises

To: **Operative A** (Lead Operative)

From: **Dr Alpha Bett,** NICE Director
and the world's greatest criminal
mastermind (dictated to and typed by
Cassie Nova, new PA to Dr Alpha Bett)

Date: July 2 (17 days remaining)

Time is getting short. I know your
plan is in place and building up to
the wedding on July 18 but this is
making me nervous AND I DO NOT LIKE
BEING NERVOUS.

Do you know how tiring it is being
bait for Agents Bubble and Squeak?

Get on with your mission and GET ME
THOSE MISSILE CODES!

If I don't have the codes in time for
the **World Leaders' Summit on July
19**, I will not be responsible for my
actions!

Oh, and by the way, when this is over,
do you want your own ten-year-old to
look after? You're getting on well
with Target 2 so you're clearly good
with children. I keep getting these
annoying, badgering letters from the
orphanage, regarding my "guardianship"
of Operative C's child until they
find Operative C. The little brat is
called Armando or Augustus or Alan or
something. I don't want him. Maybe he
can join you on your island? Another

great idea from my massive, genius
brain, yes?

Mr and Mrs Spicer
The International Federation of Sprout Farmers
11353
Outer Castonga

July 6

Dear ~~Bunny and Sterling~~ ~~Mum and Dad~~ Bunny and Sterling.

Something AWFUL happened today - someone broke into
our house!

   Me and Grandad were out all day at the "Competition
of the Choirs" (which we won, by the way - apparently the
judges were impressed because no choir from our age
group had ever had someone singing a <u>bass line</u> before!)
THEN, would you believe it, Grandad went up and asked
Miss Davis if Fleming Voices could sing for his wedding to
Mrs Allbright and she said YES! So that means Samira will

be at Grandad's wedding. ~~I'm so glad I've got a fancy new suit to wear.~~

So that part of the day was good but after we got off the bus and walked back to our house, we saw the front door was open. It was a bit scary, but nothing seems to have been taken - it's all just a big mess. Whoever it was even managed to get into that locked drawer

in your study desk (so I've been able to clear out the sponge bits and wax shavings).

Grandad took me to Mrs Allbright's so we could check she was OK and see whether she'd seen anything, but she wasn't in. As we walked back round to ours, I realized the person in the pest control van parked outside Mrs Allbright's house might have seen something, so I gave it a knock. The van suddenly started up and zoomed off down the street. I thought that was really odd but Grandad said they probably just had a sudden pest emergency to get to. I bet he's right.

Tidying up the house was a rubbish end to the day, especially after winning the choir competition. I wish you were here.

Love
Freddy ♥

P.S. I don't know why we had to get the bus to the choir competition. Harry drove a car there - we could have got a lift.

Hang on a second. Harry drove? That can't be right. He's

ten - he can't drive!

Oh my goodness.

I know exactly what is going on.

I don't believe it.

Harry ...

Is ...

So lucky!

He's got one of those new, fancy driverless cars! Can he BE

any more cool?

National

Institute for

Criminal

Enterprises

To: **Dr Alpha Bett**, Director

From: **Operative A** (Lead Operative)

Date: July 7 (12 days remaining)

Mission: Missile Code Retrieval

Is the world's greatest criminal
mastermind feeling a bit nervous?
Does the world's greatest criminal
mastermind need a hug? Do not worry,
Dr Bett — when have I ever let you
down? Everything is under control and
on track.

The house searches have proved
unsuccessful but I am not a one trick

pony — this pony can do many, many tricks! Surely that's why you needed my expertise is this suburban hell-hole?

Target 2 <u>will</u> help me track down the missile codes — the silly boy will do ANYTHING to be taken to "Blast Yourself Bonkers". It's sweet, really. But when this is all over, he will get blasted — to smithereens!

So no, I will have had quite enough of ten-year-old boys after this mission without taking on Operative C's child. YOU were named as guardian. You have to step up and take responsibility.

Mr and Mrs Spicer
The International Federation of Sprout Farmers
11353
Outer Castonga

July 8

Dear Bunny and Sterling,

DISASTER!

Mrs Allbright came round all upset and teary. She's been

looking all over for ... GRANDAD'S PASSPORT!!

So that's her surprise - she wants to take Grandad on

honeymoon!! Mrs Allbright said she needs me to be her

special wedding helper <u>right now</u> and help find the special

secret hiding place of Grandad's passport. She said if

she couldn't find it then they wouldn't be able to go on

honeymoon so there wouldn't be any point in having the

wedding.

OH NO! I thought - If there's no wedding, there'll be no

BLAST YOURSELF BONKERS for me.

WE MUST FIND THAT PASSPORT!!!!

Mrs Allbright said that things like passports are kept in

very SAFE places and could I think of any SAFE place in the

house where you might keep things SAFE.

OH

MY

GOODNESS

BRAINWAVE!!!

What if Grandad did ACTUALLY SEE a SPECIAL SECRET SAFE *behind* Dad's favourite painting? I'll have to tell Mrs Allbright about this first thing in the morning.

Ha! The trip to *BLAST YOURSELF BONKERS* is so close I can taste it!!!

EXCITING!!!!!!!

love

Freddy

P.S. Maybe sprouts are making me super clever coz I've just had another brainwave. I can't believe I haven't thought of this before! I'm going to write to your boss about the wedding! *Right now.* What a brilliant idea! If anyone can get you home from Outer Castonga in time for Grandad's wedding, it is Sir Mustard-Greens.

Sir L. Mustard-Greens
Director
The International Federation of ~~Stinky~~ Sprout Farmers
Mayfair
London

July 8

Dear Sir Mustard-Greens,

Can you let my mum and dad (Bunny and Sterling Spicer) come back from Outer Castonga for Grandad's wedding, please?

The wedding is on July 18 so time is running out and Mum and Dad haven't answered any of my letters for ages. I'm not even sure they're getting mine in the post any more.

Grandad is marrying Mrs Allbright. She's really old but

198

so is he, so that's OK. And if the wedding goes well, Mrs

Allbright will take me to *BLAST YOURSELF BONKERS*.

So you see how important it is for Mum and Dad to come

back.

Thanks

~~Love~~

Sincerely

Freddy

P.S. Please stop sending us sprouts.

Comms from Sir Mustard-G

Protection Agent Desiree and
Agent Bean (AKA Harry Covair)

Valued Agents,

What should arrive on my desk this
morning but a missive from Freddy
Spicer himself. Imagine my surprise
and consternation. I nearly choked
on my Earl Grey!

Who is Mrs Allbright? Should one
be concerned about the wedding
Freddy mentions? Why does he think
his parents haven't been receiving
his letters? And what, in the name
of Fortnum and Mason, is "Blast
Yourself Bonkers"? It sounds
utterly frightful.

S (HEAD OF IEA/IFSF) JULY 9

CERTAINLY, WE CAN ASSUME THAT
HE'S MISTAKEN ABOUT THE LETTERS,
AS I KNOW YOU, DESIREE, HAVE THIS
IN HAND. I HAVE NO DOUBT THAT OUR
STELLAR SPROUT COVER STORY IS STILL
INTACT BUT SOME REASSURANCE FROM
YOU BOTH WILL HELP EASE MY MIND
REGARDING THE ABOVE MATTERS.

I AWAIT YOUR RESPONSES WITH GREAT
ANTICIPATION.

Mr and Mrs Spicer
The International Federation of Sprout Farmers
11353
Sprouter Castonga

July 9

Dear Bunny and Sterling,

I WAS RIGHT!!!

   I told Mrs Allbright about what Grandad had said about a
safe in the lounge this morning. We took down the painting
and there it was!!! Mrs Allbright was really pleased with
me.

   But it needs a code to get in. A five-number code. I tried
all our birthdays but they didn't work. Mrs Allbright said
she was sure I would be able think of five numbers that

were important to the family in some way. She said that, given some time, I'll come up with it. *Especially* if I wanted to go to *BLAST YOURSELF BONKERS* .

She told me to sleep on it. She's RELYING on me and says she knows I can do it. She says I HAVE THE ANSWER!!

Oh dear, what if I let her down? I don't think I can stand missing out on *BLAST YOURSELF BONKERS* again. I have to work it out!!

If only I wasn't so rubbish at numbers! *MAGICAL MONSTER MATHS* has been USELESS!

I don't think I'll sleep well tonight! The only way I could get that code is if YOU give me the answer. I keep thinking of ideas of how I could get an answer from you. I have made a list:

- Send an email. But there is no internet service in Outer Castonga. So I would have to set up the internet to Outer Castonga. Too difficult.

- Phone call. Phones in Outer Castonga are really unreliable so that won't work. I did think I could try ringing Sir Mustard-Greens at the International Federation of Sprout Farmers but I cannot find a phone number for it anywhere.

- Invent a transporter to get myself to Outer Castonga. The journey would be quick but I don't know how long it would take for me to invent a transporter.

- Send a message by super-speedy pigeon. I did look out into the street to see if I could spot one, but I don't think I've actually seen any around since Harry frazzled one with my blaster.

My only hope is that you are on your way back right now. Maybe my letter to your boss worked and you'll walk through the front door tomorrow morning and all of my problems will be solved!

love

Freddy

P.S. I asked Mrs Allbright what would happen to me when her and Grandad go on honeymoon but she said I don't need to worry about that and *I will be taken care of.* Good old Mrs Allbright. She's thinking of everything!

National

Institute for

Criminal

Enterprises

To: **Dr Alpha Bett**, Director

From: **Operative A** (Lead Operative)

Date: July 9 (10 days remaining)

Mission: Missile Code Retrieval

REQUEST: A visit from Operative E, AKA

"the professional"

Mr and Mrs Spicer
The International Federation of Cheese Makers
ONLY JOKING!!
The International Federation of Sprout Farmers
11353
Outer Castonga

July 10

Dear Bunny and Sterling,

There was an eye-test for my class at school today! The
teachers must have forgotten it was going to happen coz
the eye doctor person turned up and NO ONE had been
expecting her. Mr Norbert was not pleased to have his
lesson disturbed and the school secretary had to move
out of her office for the eye doctor to work in it instead.
Everyone got to go ahead of me. Everyone except Harry,
who they'd forgotten to put on the register. It was really
boring waiting.

When it was my turn, the eye doctor asked me to read from a lot of letters. But I must have failed the test or something (maybe you were right, Dad, and I have been sitting too close to the telly) coz she shut the door and got me to wear some very strange glasses. She told me to stare into this black-and-white spinning thing. I started

to feel sleepy. I must have looked sleepy too coz the eye doctor kept saying, "You are feeling sleepy. You are feeling sleepy." over and over again. Then she asked me to think of a five-digit number - to picture a five-digit safe number in my head.

Next thing I knew, Harry barged in and shoved me out the door. He must have got *really* bored and annoyed waiting for his turn to interrupt like that. SO RUDE!

I waited outside the room for Harry. I heard some yelling, so he must have been <u>really</u> cross at being left till the end. Then there was LOTS of banging and crashing. When Harry came out of the room, the eye doctor must have already left another way coz there was no sign of her or her equipment. I do wonder why Harry walked out with the office rug rolled up over his shoulder, though.

love

freddy

COMMS FROM PROTE

REPORT TO SIR MUSTARD-GREENS (HEAD
OF IEA/IFSF)
JULY 11

SIR, I AM CONCERNED THAT AGENT BEAN
HAS "GONE ROGUE".

AS I HAVE CONTINUED TO REPORT,
THERE IS NOTHING SUSPICIOUS TO
INVESTIGATE OR ACT ON. EVERYTHING
WITH FREDDY AND MR SPICER SENIOR
HAS BEEN FINE *UNTIL* AGENT BEAN
TURNED UP.

YESTERDAY, AGENT BEAN ATTACKED AN
INNOCENT EYE DOCTOR AT FREDDY'S
SCHOOL! HE IS TAKING HIS ROLE
AS FREDDY'S PROTECTOR FAR TOO

ON AGENT DESIREE

SERIOUSLY AND IS PUTTING THE IFSF COVER STORY IN JEOPARDY. THERE ARE NO PROBLEMS OTHER THAN THE ONES AGENT BEAN IS CAUSING. REMEMBER SPORTS DAY? WHAT KIND OF AGENT REVEALS HIS COVER TO A TEACHER? DO WE REALLY NEED HIM ON THIS MISSION? HE IS IN DANGER OF RUINING EVERYTHING.

AS DAMAGE LIMITATION, SEND MORE SPROUTS!

National

Institute for

Criminal

Enterprises

To: **Dr Alpha Bett**, Director

From: **Operative A** (Lead Operative)

Date: July 12 (7 days remaining)

Mission: Missile Code Retrieval

Operative E (AKA "The Professional")
appears to have vanished. Only time
will tell if Target 2 is responding
to Operative E's treatment. Have
patience.

For future missions, we must review
approaches to dealing with school
children and put in place proper
training and preparation. Children

are terrifying and test even the most experience operatives! Maybe, when you take on responsibility for Operative C's child, you will learn this for yourself!

Mr and Mrs Spicer
The International Federation of Sprout Farmers
11353
Outer Castonga

July 13

Dear Bunny and Sterling,

I've just had a VERY STRANGE WEEKEND.

There's less than a week to go until the wedding and all I
can think about is NUMBERS!

Five days to go means there's
113 hours - or 6,780 minutes, if
you prefer - as I'm writing this
at six p.m. on Monday and the
wedding will be at eleven a.m.

on Saturday. You see? Numbers! Numbers! Numbers!

On Sunday, I could suddenly remember all the questions in the maths test - and I KNEW the right answers!! I wrote them down to show Mr Norbert (and I made doubly-sure to write the answers NOT with that stupid sprout pen) but he wouldn't look at them - it was like he was already on holiday.

Everything at school is finishing up. This means Harry won't be around for much longer, I guess. We've even cleaned out our trays. No more *MAGICAL MONSTER MATHS* (not that I need that any more!) or any after-school club - EXCEPT choir rehearsals are STILL going on, thanks to Grandad and the wedding. Lamont Riley is annoyed about it coz all he wants to do is play football in the park after school. Grandad has

215

asked Miss Davis if Fleming Voices can sing a new song - one he's picked out especially for Mrs Allbright.

Grandad is dead chuffed he's got the school choir singing but he's also FINALLY told me where he's having the wedding... He's having it AT MY SCHOOL!!!!! Poor Mrs Allbright! She's always talking about going to dead glamorous places like the Ritz. Fleming School is probably the least glamorous place I can think of! Grandad's even booked the school caterers so the wedding meal will be something

SOGGY   HARD

like soggy chicken nuggets and hard potatoes. At least Desiree will be there to help serve the guests - it will be nice to have her around.

Grandad's asked the choir to sing as Mrs Allbright arrives into the playground and also when they leave. This

216

is brilliant!! I've realized this means that everyone in the choir will see my funny trick with the motorbike, sidecar and SPROUTS. Ah ha, another brilliant idea has just come to mind... I might add some of those old fireworks from the shed into my trick too, so things will ~~defimately~~ definitely go with A BANG!!! That way, I'll end the year known as the funniest kid in school - result!

Please try and make it back. Did you hear from Sir Mustard-Greens?

Love

Freddy

P.S. Even though I'm thinking of numbers ALL THE TIME now, I still haven't worked out the five numbers I need for the safe. It is SO frustrating and stressful. Grrrrrhhhh!

P.P.S. I would give ANYTHING for some Ma Teeny's Chocolate Milk right now - that would calm me down. But there's still half the tub of Budget Boris's Chocolate-flavour Drink left. That's about forty litres of lumpy-carpet-tea-breath-liquid. which, I've worked out. will take me about fourteen years. three months and twelve days to get through because it is SO DISGUSTING!

P.P.P.S. There's now 6,752 minutes to go till the wedding.

Agent Bean report to IFSF/IEA

July 13

I can't help feeling something isn't
right. I am beginning to suspect
that Desiree is not all she seems.
Why does she keep insisting that
everything is fine when there
have been several very suspicious
incidents over the last few weeks?
I will be on full alert during the
wedding as it is my duty, as Freddy's
protector, to help in whatever way
necessary.

AGENTS HAVE A PHARAOH WAY TO GO TO CATCH DR ALPHA BETT

The famous Great Pyramid at Giza became part of the story of the infamous Dr Alpha Bett today as the self-styled criminal mastermind appeared there before shocked crowds.

Wearing a white suit and his trademark A-Z gold chains, Dr Bett dazzled in the Egyptian sun. He calmly walked, undisturbed, around the ancient site, looking like he didn't have a care in the world. However, when two "living statues" moved from their plinths and started to approach Dr Bett, he jumped on a dune buggy that he had stashed close by and zoomed off, leaving the painted people to eat his dust.

Who were these living statues? According to eyewitnesses, one was dressed as Tutankhamun and the other as Cleopatra. Can this male/female pairing be evidence that they were the same couple who have been present at each of the Dr Bett sightings? The International Espionage Agency is still unavailable for comment.

Mr and Mrs Spicer
The International Federation of Sprout Farmers
11353
Outer Castonga

July 15

Dear Bunny and Sterling,

Last night I kept thinking about numbers. They're all I can

think about since that eye test. I keep dreaming of those

swirling patterns going round and round and round and ...

... while I was sleeping, it came to me ...

TA-DA! Hero Freddy!

I have saved the honeymoon, the wedding and,

most importantly,

BLAST YOURSELF BONKERS !

The five-digit number for the safe is : 11353

11353! Of course! The number I've been writing down in letters to you for months! The postcode for the International Federation of Sprout Farmers in Outer Castonga!!

As soon as I woke up, the answer was in my head. I tried it and - click - it worked!!

In the safe were three passports: Grandad's (phew - the honeymoon can happen so the wedding can happen so BYB can happen. Hooray!!!), mine and an extra one.

The third passport looked like a normal passport from the outside but inside was REALLY weird - there wasn't even a photo in it! The passport was for a "Miss Ile Code". Who is she? And why is her passport full of so many strange numbers? I checked my passport and it's nothing like that!

Mrs Allbright was dead pleased when I told her about the passports and she told me I was a superstar because "everything can now go as planned". Of course. I've locked all the passports back up for now - I don't know why but Mrs Allbright seemed annoyed about this. It is only sensible to keep passports safe until they're actually needed.

Wow. Because I found the passport, the wedding can go smoothly and Mrs Allbright will not be a Bridezilla. I will get to go to *BLAST YOURSELF BONKERS* and hopefully you will be back for the wedding! It's like all my wishes ever are coming true.

Yours excitedly

Love

Freddy

P.S. Jordan Fishwick came round after school. He looked awful - all scared and weepy. I almost felt sorry for him. He brought back the red phone, whimpering. "WHAT ARE YOUR POSITIONS, AGENT BUBBLE AND AGENT SQUEAK? KEEP THE CODE SAFE!" He sounds like he's believing his own crazy lies!!!

National

Institute for

Criminal

Enterprises

To: **Dr Alpha Bett**, Director

From: **Operative A** (Lead Operative)

Date: July 16 (3 days remaining)

Mission: Missile Code Retrieval

Objective achieved!

I *told* you my plan would work!

I *told* you to have patience!

I *told* you to trust me!

Exact location of Missile Codes

identified.

I can't quite believe how long it's taken or how many NICE resources we've had to use — but it's all been worth it to get to this point.

Target 2 was interfering again so I was unable to actually GET the codes — but I know where they are AND how to get them. Awaiting the go-ahead from you.

Permission to leave and NOT go through with wedding to Target 1?

To: **Operative A** (Lead Operative)

From: **Dr Alpha Bett**, NICE Director

and the world's greatest criminal

mastermind (dictated to and typed by

Cassie Nova, new PA to Dr Alpha Bett)

Date: July 16 (3 days remaining)

Operative A: WELL DONE. My brilliance

has enabled you to achieve the mission

objective.

Yes, you have my permission to get the

codes and get out of there.

I have one last trick up my sleeve to

distract Agents Bubble and Squeak, to prevent any last-minute problems. After that, I will make my way to Jakarta. I will meet you at the World Leaders' Summit.

My quest is nearly over. WORLD DOMINATION is within my grasp. By this time on Sunday, all the leaders in the world will have given over ALL POWER TO ME! Ha ha ha ha ha ha

Mr and Mrs Spicer
The International Federation of Sprout Farmers
11353
Outer Castonga

July 17

Dear Bunny and Sterling,

Just call me THE SUPER-MEGA WEDDING SAVER!

Last night I was doing all the final preparations for the

wedding. I was wearing my new suit (to make sure I hadn't

grown too much and to get rid of

some of the ~~wierd~~ odd creases) and

when I looked in the mirror - BAM! -

I realized I looked like an amazingly

cool and ~~sofisticated~~ sophisticated

spy! Then I remembered I had to go

to Mrs Allbright's shed to sort out my HILARIOUS PRANK
for the wedding (stuffing all those leftover sprouts in the
sidecar - tee hee!) so I got properly into character and
started making the best spy moves I could think of! I slinked
down our hallway and dodged around the kitchen before
sneaking out into the garden and sidling along the fence.
I even managed a commando roll over into Mrs Allbright's
shed - I hope I haven't dirtied my suit too much!

In the shed the old motorbike and sidecar looks very
smart. I have to admit. Grandad has done a good job. But
when Grandad asks Mrs Allbright to step into the sidecar
after they're married. she'll just find it full of sprouts. (I
counted 1,862 sprouts, just at one glance as I tipped them
in!) I've also hidden a couple of the old shed fireworks in the
sidecar, which I will take out and set off in the playground
when Grandad and Mrs Allbright are ready to leave. It will

make a spectacular send-off!!!

Suddenly, when I was in the shed, my super-spy senses kicked in and I looked over to Mrs Allbright's place. I saw Mrs Allbright frantically packing up her house. I guess she'll live with us after the wedding.

I popped round to say hello.

Mrs Allbright's front door was open and in the hallway were five – FIVE – big suitcases! Goodness, she must be taking a lot of stuff on her honeymoon. And on the hall table were the passports – she must have gone back to the safe to get them when I wasn't around. Fair enough. I wanted to see Mrs Allbright's age coz she's so ancient – so I had a sneaky peak at her passport. Her first name is Operative! Operative Allbright. What a strange name! Maybe it's an old family name?

231

But – AND MOST IMPORTANT AND WHY I AM TOTALLY THE BEST WEDDING SAVER EVER – she must have picked up the wrong passport coz, instead of Grandad's, she had the one for Miss Code.

OH NO! I thought. Mrs Allbright hadn't seen me so I snuck back to our house, got Grandad's passport and did a switcheroo!!! Super-spy Freddy to the rescue!

I have saved the day and no one knows about it (except you). Mrs Allbright was right to ask me to be her *special wedding helper*, wasn't she?

So everything is prepared and ready (thanks to me).
Will you be there? Fingers and toes crossed!!

Love

Freddy

P.S. OH NO! I've just realized I'm going to have to watch Grandad and Mrs Allbright KISS at the registry office. That might be EVEN MORE yucky than sprouts!

DR BETT'S PAINFUL END?

The Summer Olympics, watched by millions around the globe for their world-class athletics, became the focus of the world today for completely different reasons. During the archery contest, the crowds gasped as a new contestant, dressed all in white and wearing A-Z gold chains, approached the archery range. A hushed crowd watched as Dr Alpha Bett raised his bow – but before he could aim at the target, two other unidentified archers (one male, one female) ran on to the range – a move totally illegal in any kind of competitive archery! Dr Bett quickly loosed his arrow at the male archer before starting to walk calmly out of the stadium. However, the female archer, in an impressive move that would not have been out of place in the gymnastics competition, dived in front of the arrow and deflected it with her hand. Despite visible injury, the female archer then shot her own arrow at the retreating Dr Bett. As Dr Bett left the stadium, he was heard to shout, "Ouch, my bottom!" and the crowd cheered the anonymous archers.

There was not even any point asking the International Espionage Agency for comment.

Hi Freddy,

We think our work is about to finish — isn't that exciting? We should warn you that Mummy has hurt her hand on a sharp piece of sprout _equipment_. 'Tis a nasty scratch but it will hopefully have healed by the time we return — we just don't want you to worry if it is still in a bandage when you see us. Who knew _sprout farming_ was so dangerous!!

Looking forward to seeing you.

Love and Hugs
Mummy and Daddy

Freddy Spicer
61 Bond Lane
Fleming
Flemingshire
BR0 Ct1

Olympic Opening Ceremonies through the years

235

COMMS FROM SIR MUSTARD

TO PROTECTION AGENT DESIREE AND
AGENT BEAN (AKA HARRY COVAIR)
JULY 17

ESTEEMED AGENTS,

NOW IS NOT A TIME TO POINT FINGERS
AND ACCUSE EACH OTHER. SUSPICION
AND FEAR ARE PRECISELY WHAT THAT
ROTTER, DR ALPHA BETT, IS WANTING
US TO FEEL. WE MUST UNITE AND WORK
TOGETHER TO ENSURE AGENT BUBBLE
AND SQUEAK'S FAMILY ARE PROTECTED
DURING THIS TIME OF HEIGHTENED
THREAT FROM THE BRUTISH MISCREANT.

PUT ASIDE YOUR DIFFERENCES. YOU
MUST BRUSH YOURSELVES DOWN, TAKE
AN INVIGORATING BATH (IT ALWAYS HELPS

EENS (HEAD OF IEA/IFSF)

ME – I'LL SEND OVER MY PERSONAL
RECIPE OF EPSOM SALTS, LAVENDER OIL
AND ROSE PETALS) AND BE READY TO
PROCEED ONCE MORE UNTO THE BREACH.

WHEN THIS TIRESOME NONSENSE IS
ALL OVER, I WILL BE READY WITH THE
MOST VIGOROUS OF HANDSHAKES,
THE HEARTIEST OF PATS ON THE
BACK AND, FOR GOOD MEASURE, AN
EFFUSIVE RUFFLE OF YOUR HAIR, TO
CONGRATULATE YOU BOTH FOR A JOB
WELL DONE.

Mr and Mrs Spicer
The International Federation of Sprout Farmers
11353
Outer Castonga

July 18 - morning

Dear Bunny and Sterling,

I can't believe you're missing the big day. ~~I really thought~~
~~you'd make it back. Grandad is going to be gutted too. I~~
~~keep looking at the door, thinking you'll walk through it any~~
~~second~~ we're all gathered at school, waiting. Just waiting
is *really* boring.

It's hard to breathe with this tie on. I do like my new suit,
though, and still feel a bit spy-like whenever I see myself in
a mirror. It's almost like having a super power! I keep trying
to raise one eyebrow like I've seen spies do in movies but

238

I'm rubbish at it. I bet, with his eyebrows, Lamont would be awesome at doing the ~~swarve~~ suave eyebrow thing. I've got the wedding rings in my suit pocket, so I feel dead important. I've also realized I forgot to put Miss Code's passport back in the safe - that's in my pocket too.

Grandad looks all fancy, standing at the front of the school hall in his new suit. He looks so smart that hopefully Mrs Allbright will forgive him about the motorbike and sidecar - I can't see her enjoying that! But Grandad is sooo proud of it. It's parked right outside the school entrance, where the choir will be singing when Mrs Allbright eventually turns up. At least she can enjoy my HILARIOUS prank, though.

The school hall looks cleaner than I've ever seen it but Grandad should maybe have spent more on flowers and decorations coz it does just look like, well, a school hall! There's a smell of over-boiled vegetables coming from the canteen.

Harry is now standing at the back of the room looking all cool and serious in his sunglasses. He's not wearing a suit, just some trousers and a shirt, but the shirt looks really tiny. His muscles are bursting out and the neck button won't even do up! Maybe Harry's dad hasn't had chance to go shopping since Harry's growth-spurt. When will I have my growth spurt?

Actually - _one_ interesting thing has happened while we've been waiting! Desiree came out from the canteen, probably to check how I am because she's so lovely and caring. She should have left the chopping knife in the kitchen - I'd have thought that would have been covered in her dinner lady training! Anyway, instead of coming to me,

she headed for Harry! He saw her and started fiddling
with his cufflinks. GUESS WHAT? He has EXACTLY the same
cufflinks as you, Dad. You know, the cufflinks decorated
with sprouts? Anyway, as Desiree got closer, I heard a *POP*,
Fzzzzzzz – oh dear, had Grandad farted at his own wedding?
Probably the nerves! Suddenly (probably out of shock and
disgust) Desiree slumped to the floor! Harry finally stopped

fiddling with his cufflinks then and carried Desiree to a
chair. He's so strong! Now Desiree's snoring away like
she'll sleep for days. She probably doesn't get enough sleep,
what with all those midnight walks.

Other than that excitement, I've been trying to fill the boring time by attempting to take some photos using the camera I found in my Docs while we've been waiting, but I can't work out how to get my foot in the right position to take a good shot <u>and</u> press the clicker. A camera in a shoe is a bit of a rubbish idea. Got lots of pictures of the hall's floor, though.

As best man and guest, me and Harry have had to wait inside. But the rest of Fleming Voices are ready and positioned on the steps, waiting to burst into song when Mrs Allbright arrives. Lamont is going to shout when she pulls up so me and Harry can go join them. I can't wait to get outside and see Samira. I caught a glimpse of her when she first got here and her hair is even more glossy than ever. Jordan is outside too. He's turned up with his new camera – I hope he doesn't try to push Mrs Allbright over to get new viral video footage to put online. But maybe he'll take a good video of the fireworks going off. I can't wait to see what a Military Grade Grenade looks like! Argh, that reminds me. I should have got them out of the sidecar already. Must do that when I finish this letter.

Mrs Allbright is taking AAAAAAAAAGGGGGGEEEESSSSS to arrive. Grandad's said it's traditional for a bride to be late. Boring boring waiting.

OOOooooh - A car's screeched up outside. I bet that's Mrs Allbright. Yep - Lamont's foghorn voice has just sounded. Wedding is go! Will write more later.

love

Freddy

Mr and Mrs Spicer
The International Federation of Sprout Farmers
11353
Outer Castonga

July 18 - evening

Dear Bunny and Sterling,

What a day!

Do you know, after waiting around for so long, I thought
it was going to be mega boring but it was ACTION-PACKED
and I have learnt three important things:

1) Bridezillas are terrifying! (Dad was right!)

Mrs Allbright turned up massively late in full-on BRIDEZILLA
MODE, driving a super-speedy car like a maniac. Mrs
Allbright clearly got dressed in a real hurry coz her
wedding dress was on backwards and her make-up was

scribbled all over her face, like a toddler had tried to make

her look like a panda in lipstick. Being a Bridezilla must send

you completely loony!

Harry and I joined the choir and started singing "*You*

are so beautiful", but it was difficult for Fleming Voices to

be heard coz Mrs Allbright was shouting the place down –

she was even louder than Lamont!

She kept shouting "Where is the passport? I need the

passport. You've RUINED the plan!" How barmy is that? I

have no idea what she was on about but she looked right at

me. How could Mrs Allbright think I'd ruined the wedding

when I'd SAVED it?

I tried to keep singing with the choir, coz Grandad had

picked the song specially, but Mrs Allbright got a *crazy*

look in her eye. She started coming
towards me in a really scary-
looking way. Suddenly, Harry
did a mega flying rugby
tackle at her from the steps
but Mrs Allbright again did
that awesome jump-dive into
a commando roll that she did
at my party. I wonder where
she learnt to do that? Harry <u>missed</u> Mrs Allbright and
instead went <u>head-first</u> into the super-speedy car. I think
he knocked himself out. Just his legs were sticking out of
the car. Poor Harry - he was trying to be super brave!

The choir stopped singing by this point so I tried to tell
Mrs Allbright I was just being her *special wedding helper*.
That did not seem to help and I was actually feeling quite

scared by this point so I tried to run away from her but that made my Docs go PING CLICK and out popped A SHARP SPIKE from the front of the left shoe. Why would Doctor Martin put a spike in a shoe, Mum? Doesn't he realize it's REALLY dangerous? I didn't want to hurt anyone with it so I couldn't really move anywhere and Mrs Bridezilla Allbright caught up with me. She shoved me into the sidecar and started up the motorbike.

I know Grandad was dead proud of putting together the motorbike and sidecar for the wedding but it was *really* uncomfortable in the sidecar coz I'd filled it with all those leftover sprouts (1,857 of them – five sprouts got speared on my toe-spike). So my great plan for a prank on Mrs Allbright became a prank ON ME!

As the motorbike lurched forward, Mrs Allbright was muttering. *"Why couldn't you just have stopped meddling? Then everything would have been OK. All I wanted was the passport!"*

Then I remembered - Miss Code's passport was IN MY SUIT POCKET! Well, I thought, if Mrs Allbright wanted it that much, I didn't see any harm in giving it to her. ANYTHING to calm her down!

I tried to get the passport out, which was not easy because the space was really tight and my knees were up round my ears. As I was squirming to get to my pocket, I accidentally hit a big red button in the sidecar, which brings me to the next thing I learnt today:

2) Never trust anything Grandad has put together.

Grandad had worked <u>SO HARD</u> on putting the sidecar and motorbike together but he must have wired the whole thing up wrong – coz when I caught that red button with my elbow, the whole thing suddenly went...

The motorbike, sidecar, me and Mrs Allbright were flying through the air.

ACTUALLY FLYING!

We were off like a rocket! I was so surprised that I dropped Miss Code's passport somewhere in all the sprouts.

We passed the school hall windows and roof and suddenly everyone below was looking very small. I calculated we were twenty metres high in just half a second, meaning we were accelerating at 160 metres per second SQUARED!! A motorbike and sidecar shouldn't do that!! Silly Grandad.

I tried to keep cool - I was dressed like a spy, after all - so I thought to myself what a spy would do and decided to press a different button and

KER-POING!

I have to say, Grandad might have wired it wrong but I'm well impressed he put in

EJECTOR SEATS!!!!!

My chair sprang out of the sidecar and shot through the air BY ITSELF!! Suddenly, a parachute shot out the back of my chair. It was while I was floating back down to earth that I learnt my last important lesson of the day:

3) Things don't always go to plan.

As I floated, the motorbike and sidecar went...

There was a MASSIVE explosion!!!!

My fireworks went off!!

Lights glittered and sparkled across the sky and exploded the sprouts I'd put in the sidecar - all 1,857 of them! Lots of little green bits fluttered down to the ground. It was BEAUTIFUL!!! I hope Mrs Allbright liked it. I never saw where her ejector seat landed.

I was hit in the forehead by a flying white shoe like Mrs Allbright was wearing and that's the last thing I remember. I'm writing this from hospital. People keep telling me I'm fine and have been a very brave boy.

I know I have been brave because I haven't cried at all - even though there was NO ACTUAL WEDDING so that means Mrs Allbright won't be taking me to *BLAST YOURSELF BONKERS*

That is rubbish.

Love

Freddy

WORLD LEADERS' SUMMIT IN JAKARTA HAILED A "GREAT SUCCESS"

The eyes of the world were on Jakarta today, as key world leaders converged for the World Leaders' Summit. Security was at its highest level for Dr Alpha Bett, still at large, surely wouldn't pass up an opportunity like this for mayhem?

As the last session of the summit drew to a close, there was a sudden shout from the conference floor – and Dr Bett, dressed in his trademark white suit and A-Z gold chains, approached the podium. Dr Bett announced he was about to be in possession of missile codes and intended to hold the world to ransom. Allowing his words to sink in with delegates, Dr Bett sat down triumphantly – with a wince as his injured bottom made contact with a chair. Silence fell over the summit as, for several minutes, Dr Bett alternated between staring at the conference hall doors and checking his phone.

Keen to return to their home countries, delegates, one-by-one, started leaving. As the last of the delegates emptied out of the great conference hall, Dr Bett continued to sit and wait for someone who never turned up. He was such a pitiful figure, security services didn't even have the heart to arrest him. Dr Bett was allowed to slink away. Is this the end for the self-styled world's greatest criminal mastermind?

To: **Operative D** (Sleeper Operative)

From: **Dr Alpha Bett,** NICE Director

and the world's greatest criminal

mastermind (dictated to and typed by

Cassie Nova, new PA to Dr Alpha Bett)

Date: July 20 (-1 days remaining)

MISSION FAILED

Operative D: what is your position?

Operative A is not responding to any

messages and is presumed no longer

active. She promised she'd meet me in

Jakarta. I waited and waited. I knew

I shouldn't have put all my trust in

her!

Report back, Operative D. It's me and you now. Time to stop being a sleeper undercover operative.

Please report back.

Would you like your own private island?

This is all just a minor set-back. I will rise again — you just wait! And you'll want to be at my side when the time comes!

I am, after all, the world's greatest criminal mastermind.

Sniff.

But, for now, I can't even sit down

properly. Oh, my bottom really hurts!

Sniff.

What am I going to do? Sniff, sniff.

No ideas left. Sniff, sniff, sniff.

I can't believe my best opportunity to achieve world domination was foiled by an idiotic child! Sniff.

How did this happen? Sniff.

How could the world's greatest criminal mastermind be bested by a ten-year-old? Sniff. Sob.

What do I know of ten-year-olds? Sob. Sob.

Hang on a tick. Sniff.

That's it! Sniff.

Well done, my beautiful big brain!

I DO have a ten-year-old at my
disposal. Operative C's child is just
waiting for his legal guardian to look
after him. That's me! This is a sign!
I will rise again! Sniff.

What? Sniff.

No I do not WANT A TISSUE! Sniff.
Are you still typing? Sniff.
Stop it! Stop typing at onc

Mr and Mrs Spicer
The International Federation of Sprout Farmers
11353
Outer Castonga

July 20

Dear Bunny and Sterling,

I'm still in hospital. I don't know why. I only got a little
bump on the head. It's really boring here. More boring
than waiting for a wedding to start.

I haven't been allowed to watch or read anything. I did
see a picture of Mrs Allbright on the telly in my neighbour's
room but someone quickly closed the curtains. I bet they
were watching *Best Ever Bridezilla Moments from Hell!* I
hope Mrs Allbright will be OK. I did like her.

Only Grandad's been allowed to visit. I think he must be a bit sad about Mrs Allbright and the wedding. He said Mrs Hubbard from down the street cooked him a lovely roast last night. I'm glad Grandad has someone looking after him! I still had the wedding rings but Grandad asked for them back - he said he might be needing them some day. I think he'll be fine.

And guess what he told me? You'll be so proud of me!! I have made SPROUTS COOL!

Jordan's video of the sprout explosion went properly viral on the internet (I guess you won't have seen it in Outer Castonga). Now everyone wants exploding sprout confetti at their weddings! So I am the inventor of the new, super-green wedding must-have!! I have called it Pongfetti!

I'm leaving hospital tomorrow, which is good because lots

259

of people want to speak the Pongfetti inventor!!

Love

Freddy

P.S. Even though he couldn't actually visit me, I did see Harry sitting outside my room day and night. Although I could see that he was drinking black coffee to stay awake. I really don't think a ten-year-old should drink black coffee – you told me it would stop me from growing. Actually, Harry is soooooo tall that maybe it doesn't matter if he doesn't grow any taller.

P.P.S. I did think Desiree might try to visit me coz she's always been so kind, but Grandad said she's disappeared and not been seen since the wedding. Maybe she's still asleep in the school hall? Someone really should check.

Freddy Spicer
61 Bond Lane
Fleming
Flemingshire
BR0 CL1

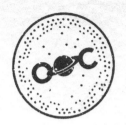

July 23

Dearest Freddy,

We're on our way home! It might take us a bit more time, but we can't wait to see you and hear about everything you have been up to over the last few months. We will be seeing our boss, Sir Mustard-Greens, soon to receive a debrief on our sprout work. Hopefully we'll also have chance to read all the letters you've been sending us – wherever they've got to! We hear from other colleagues that you have been busy with **sprouts** too. We're so proud of you!

Can't wait to give you lots of hugs and kisses.

Love
Mummy and Daddy

Mr and Mrs Spicer
The International Federation of Sprout Farmers
11353
Outer Castonga

July 28

Dear Bunny and Sterling,

I am famous!!! I have been getting calls from all kinds of
people – like journalists from "So You're Getting Married
magazine" and "Cabbage and Sprout Weekly"! I've been so
busy, I haven't even had time to miss Harry, whose time
as an exchange pupil has ended. It's amazing. Everyone is
wanting to hear about the invention of Pongfetti!

But, of course, there was only <u>one place</u> that was going
to tell my story – and one person to write it! That's right!!!
I finally got an article into the <u>school magazine</u>! I even got

on the cover! I'm the youngest ever pupil to write an article for

The Fleming Bulletin

— can you believe it!! Samira Hadid came round <u>herself</u> to drop off copies of the magazine for me so I asked her if she wanted to stay for chcolate milk but she said she needed to get home and wash her hair. ~~I don't know why - her flowing locks looked more luminous than ever.~~ I asked her if we could meet up over the holidays and Samira said she'd be washing her hair EVERY DAY. To be honest, if she's so interested in her hair, I think she might be a bit boring.

Anyway, everyone is super impressed with the article - even your boss! Yes, Sir Mustard-Greens visited me today!!

He came along with an assistant, who just stood outside while Sir Mustard-Greens gave me a medal, shook my hand like he was trying to pull it off and said I could call him "Legume". Don't posh people have weird names? The medal is all gold and shiny and there's a big sprout picture on it so I guess it's for services to sprouts. I've made them soooo popular.

I showed Sir Legume Mustard-Greens my photo on the cover of the school magazine. I thought he'd be super-pleased to read all the details I'd given about you and your work in Outer Castonga for the International Federation of Sprout Farmers. I think he was! He turned beetroot-pink and suddenly rang his assistant. He was like "Mr Sunnyhenny, we need a new cover story STRAIGHT AWAY!" I bet he wanted the story for the IFSF Newsletter!! Can you imagine me on their cover too? I bet he was secretly annoyed that **The *Fleming Bulletin*** had scooped the best sprout news in years.

    But Sir Legume Mustard-Greens seemed to feel guilty about not getting you home in time for the wedding. He said he was, "sorry I had to go through all that, what what." Then he asked lots of questions about Miss Code's passport. I told him that it had been in the sidecar when it exploded. I thought Sir Legume was going to get cross about that coz he seemed soooooooo interested in the passport - but he seemed relieved. He said it was probably a good thing it was destroyed. Just at that second, I thought back and I realized something amazing...

    I COULD REMEMBER ALL THE NUMBERS!!

    I told Sir Legume and started reciting them: "7.9.9.2.8.1.

1.3.3.3.1.0.0.1.3.2.1…"

Ever since the eye doctor visited school, I've become a right number nerd!!

Then Sir Legume Mustard-Greens went EVEN MORE BEETROOT and said something about me needing to go underground - I had no idea what he was talking about and told him I couldn't go underground because we did not have a cellar. Then he muttered something about me needing "exceptional, tip-top protection" and suddenly rushed out the door, saying he'd be back in touch VERY SOON once he's decided what will happen next. Poor man! He seemed very stressed! I hope what happens next is that you'll finally come home.

Love

Freddy

P.S. Sir Legume Mustard-Greens said he wanted to take
away ALL the COPIES of **Flemíng Bulletín**. so I
can't send one to you. but hopefully my picture above gives
you an idea of what the cover looked like.

P.P.S. I wonder if Sir Legume Mustard-Greens knows he
left his assistant behind. He's just standing outside looking
a bit bored.

URGENT COMMS FROM SIF

JULY 28

BIT OF A HEAD-SCRATCHER THIS ONE, CHAPS.
FREDDY SPICER APPEARS TO HAVE DEVELOPED
AN EXTRAORDINARY ABILITY WITH NUMBERS. I
HAVE NAMED THIS SUDDEN NUMERICAL ABILITY
PHENOMENON (SNAP). AS A MATTER OF URGENCY,
SET UP A RESEARCH STUDY INTO SNAP. FREDDY
SPICER TO BE SUBJECT #1 IN THE STUDY. HOW
HAS FREDDY GAINED THIS NEW ABILITY? AND CAN
IT BE REPLICATED? COULD SNAP BE THE FUTURE
FOR KEEPING AND DISPERSING IMPORTANT CODES?
GET TO WORK ON THE SNAP STUDY AND REPORT
BACK. PIP PIP.

UNTIL THE BOFFINS AT MISSILE HQ WORK OUT
HOW TO CHANGE THE MISSILE INITIATION CODES,
FREDDY'S KNOWLEDGE PUTS HIM IN GREAT
DANGER. I SUGGEST THAT WE PUT FREDDY
AND HIS PARENTS IN WITNESS PROTECTION

EGUME MUSTARD-GREENS

TEMPORARILY AS A PRECAUTION.

SUCH MARVELLOUS NEWS THAT AGENTS BUBBLE
AND SQUEAK ARE BACK IN THE FOLD AFTER THAT
DASTARDLY DR ALPHA BETT WAS THOROUGHLY
HUMILIATED AT THE WORLD LEADERS' SUMMIT.
SUCH A BORE HE DIDN'T ACTUALLY DO ANYTHING
ILLEGAL FOR WHICH WE COULD APPREHEND HIM.
SURELY THE BEASTLY WRETCH WILL SURFACE AGAIN
AT SOME POINT AND WE SHALL BE READY FOR HIM.
PERHAPS EVEN FREDDY HIMSELF, WITH HIS TOP-
NOTCH NEW SKILL, COULD BE A FUTURE ASSET OF
THE INTERNATIONAL ESPIONAGE AGENCY?
OH, AND MOST UNFORTUNATELY, FREDDY HAS GONE
AND BLOWN OUR SPROUT COVER ONCE AND FOR
ALL. THE HEARTIEST OF HEARTY HANDSHAKES TO
WHOMEVER COMES UP WITH A NEW COVER STORY
FOR THE INTERNATIONAL ESPIONAGE AGENCY.
ARE THERE ANY VEGETABLES WE HAVE NOT USED
YET? GET THOSE THINKING CAPS ON. QUICK AS A
WEASEL AND TWICE AS WILY. WHAT HO!

Fred-Meister
61 Bond Lane
Fleming
Flemingshire
BRO CL1

July 29

Hey Freddy,

Guess who this is?

It's AJAY!!!!!

I really wanted to write to you before now but
I've been having the most rubbish time. After Dad
went missing, I've been stuck in an orphanage. It's
been a nightmare — we had our own rooms, which
you'd think would be great but there was no telly,
no toys and we weren't allowed to talk to each

other. We didn't even have any school lessons! I have been really missing you — my last proper friend! — but the people running the orphanage wouldn't let me have pencil, paper or stamps to write to you. I hope you haven't forgotten about me.

Anyway, I thought I'd be stuck there forever — coz who wants to look after a ten-year-old boy? But then the most amazing thing happened just a few days ago...

Suddenly this person turned up who was apparently friends with my dad and he's my legal guardian. I have to call him "Doctor" and he's insisting that I wear white and this weird A-Z gold necklacey thing but I'm not complaining coz anything is better than that orphanage.

I do hope you'll write back.

Ajay

P.S. The Doctor said he didn't really like the name Coppertoe so he's called me Ajay Zincthumb instead — he likes how my first name starts with A and the last name now starts with Z. He does seem to have a bit of a thing about the alphabet. It's a bit zany but I'm cool with it.

Ajay Zincthumb
The Secret Lair
Just off Grace Bay
North Caicos

July 30

Dear Ajay,

It is sooooo awesome to hear from you. I kept hoping you'd
get in touch but I'd kind of lost hope! I did make friends
with an exchange pupil called Harry but that didn't stop me
missing you.

You sound like you've been having a rubbish time. I'm so
sorry. Sorry also about your dad - but you wouldn't believe
the crazy rumours there were around school about him. At
least you've got someone now to look after you and take
you away from that horrid orphanage. How exciting for

you! I'm so jealous you're on a proper adventure. Things here have been quite dull.

My parents have been away all this time and so I've spent loads of time just writing boring letters. While they were gone, Grandad was looking after me. He nearly married someone called Mrs Allbright. Oh, I did get to go to Hull, so that was nice. And Jordan Fishwick stopped picking on me. And I nearly won something at sports day! Maybe quite a bit has been happening after all. Like I'm really good at maths now – can you believe it? And I guess, if you've been locked away in an orphanage, you don't know about my amazing "Pongfetti" invention? Wow, so much goes on when you stop and think about it!

Mum and Dad got back a couple of days ago and it's been incredible to be with them again. They can barely stop

214

hugging me and won't let me out of their sight - it's like they think I can't look after myself or something, which is crazy coz I am ten now, of course. They totally missed my birthday (and have now taken away the awesome blaster they gave me, which is mega unfair) so they've got some making up to do. They had promised to take me to *BLAST YOURSELF BONKERS* but now I'm glad that didn't happen coz you'd have missed it.

And there is some super major news...

My parents are no longer going to be sprout farmers in Outer Castonga!!!!

They're going to be...

Turnip farming in South Maristan!

Mum and Dad's boss, Sir Legume Mustard-Greens, is concerned there's a problem with leeks there. I don't know why he should be bothered about this. Leeks are SOOOO much tastier than turnips. Or sprouts! Why would you want to get rid of them? At least it sounds like it'll be an easy job!

And I won't have to write Mum and Dad lots of boring letters because, this time, I'M GOING TO BE WITH THEM!!!!!!!!!!!!!!

We're about to set off RIGHT NOW, once I've posted this! It's all happened in such a hurry, I haven't really had time to think about ANYTHING. Grandad was going to come too but has decided to go on a WORLD CRUISE instead. Can you believe it? *Now* he decides to spend money! He's suddenly started saying things like "*Life's too short*" and "*I want to grab life by the horns*".

GRANDAD

Good for him! He's promised to send loads of postcards. I'll miss him – but I *won't* miss the vomit-inducing "Budget Boris's Chocolate-flavour Drink" he made me drink. I've snuck it into his luggage - ha ha!

Oh, and it's funny you've had your name changed. Apparently "Freddy" means something really RUDE in South Maristan (Sir Legume would not tell me what!!) so I've had to change my name too!

I'm so pleased you got in touch. Once we're settled, I promise I'll write more. And maybe you'll even be able to visit at some point? Promise you'll visit! That would be so cool because the absolutely best news is ...

drumroll please ...

(I've already checked)

... there is a *BLAST YOURSELF BONKERS* over there!!! HOORAY!

We're going to have

SO

MUCH

FUN!!!!!

Love, your new pen pal,

~~Freddy~~ Miguel

Should this be here? I don't think it's anything to do with my book. What is this doing here? Please remove. F.

ACKNOWLEDGEMENTS ???

(who!?)

Huge thanks to Yasmin Morrissey and all the team at Scholastic for being amazing. To Jack Noel for his awesome illustrations. To Jo Williamson at Antony Harwood Ltd for all the excellent support. Thanks also to the City Lit Writing for Children gang, especially the wonderful Lou and my writing buddies Terrie, Varsha and Hannah. A special mention goes to the staff of the creche and cafe at the Waltham Forest Feel Good Centre in Walthamstow, where the majority of this book was written - thanks for giving me time and tea!

No chocolate milk!?

And thanks to all my incredible family and friends, who were too polite to question the sanity of writing a sprout-themed spy book!

YUCK!